Daughters of an Emerald Dusk

KATHERINE V. FORREST

DAUGHTERS OF AN EMERALD DUSK

alyson books
los angeles

Celebrating Twenty-Five Years

Manufactured in the United States of America.

This trade paperback original is published by Alyson Books,
P.O. Box 4371, Los Angeles, California 90078-4371.
Distribution in the United Kingdom by Turnaround Publisher Services Ltd.,
Unit 3, Olympia Trading Estate, Coburg Road, Wood Green,
London N22 6TZ England.

First edition: April 2005

05 06 07 08 09 a 10 9 8 7 6 5 4 3 2 1

ISBN 1-55583-823-5
ISBN-13 978-1-55583-823-2

Library of Congress Cataloging-in-Publication Data

Forrest, Katherine V., 1939–

Daughters of an emerald dusk / Katherine V. Forrest.—1st ed.

ISBN 1-55583-823-5 (pbk.); ISBN-13 978-1-55583-823-2

1. Women—Fiction. 2. Lesbians—Fiction. 3. Space colonies—Fiction. 4. Life on other planets—Fiction. 5. Feminist fiction. lcsh. I. Title.

PS3556.O737D38 2005

813'.54—dc22 2004062355

Credits

Cover photography by Juan Silva/Image Bank/Getty Images.
Cover design by Matt Sams.

To Jo Hercus,
for everything

ACKNOWLEDGMENTS

I am especially grateful to:

Jo Hercus, my cornerstone and best critic.

My longtime friends whose invaluable input has been part of this series from its very inception: Montserrat Fontes and Clarice Gillis.

The wonderful Cath Walker, Ph.D., friend and indispensable scientist in residence, even though that happens to be in Australia.

Nancy Corporon for her caring insights and eagle eye.

Angela Brown, editor in chief at Alyson, whose attentive work and contributions to this novel are exceptional.

Many thanks once more to all the devotees of the Unity and the world of Maternas, who have written to me over the years.

I am especially indebted to James Lovelock for his espousal of the Gaia Theory, and all his books, especially Gaia: The Practical Science of Planetary Medicine (Oxford University Press, 2000), which aided immeasurably in crystallizing the thinking of my lifetime for my own book. And to the inestimable Arthur C. Clarke, whose vision and affirmation have inspired much of my futuristic work.

THE WOMEN OF MATERNAS

Mother

Her Daughters—The Inner Circle:
Minerva—the Historian
Christa, her partner
Celeste, their daughter
Olympia—the Philosopher
Ceeley, her long ago partner
Vesta—the Psychologist
Carina, her partner
Hera—the Astrophysicist
Diana—the Geneticist
Demeter—the Meditech
Venus—the Biologist
Isis—the Mathematician

Megan—the leader of the first expedition to Maternas
Laurel—her partner
Emerald—their firstborn daughter
Esme and Adira, her daughters
Crystal—their second-born daughter
Quira and Taura, her daughters

Tara, Megan's sister, and the leader of the Unity on Earth
Joss, Tara's partner
Silke, Joss's mother
Trella, Joss's sister
Nitara and Verda, Trella's daughters
Niabi, Kaylee, Netis—daughters of Nitara and Verda

Danya, senior security officer on Maternas
Erika, a geophysicist

2205.6.01—OLYMPIA

As of this day. I embark upon my greatest adventure. For the first time in my long life I hold only the scantest concept of the future spread out before me.

We cherish the peerless days in the history of our Unity, days beyond all our dreams, each seeming more consequential than any previous…

The first, surely, the day our extraordinary, singular Mother gave birth to the original nine of our Unity—of which I am one.

The day six generations later when our Unity came to its momentous decision to abdicate all further involvement in the affairs of Earth. Seven months afterward, the day that 4,144 of our number made their clandestine departure to seek a new home in the stars.

The day following, when the 2,011 remaining on Earth—of which I am one—selected our home to be in the forbidding—and what we mistakenly thought to be safe—environs of Sappho Valley, historically known as Death Valley.

Finally, that most tumultuous day of all, the confrontation with Theo Zedera, who had spent more than two years relentlessly scouring the entire planet for us.

And now this day. Wisdom and perspective—the fruit borne out of my more than a century of life—should persuade me that proclaiming this day as the most significant of all is foolish.

Call me foolish.

Still, I swing from exhilaration to despair. If wholly uncharted terrain beckons to me, I must leave my beloved Earth to seek it; and I know not when or if I will return. Beyond that: The sister closest to me, dearest Isis, is adamant that at least one of Mother's original nine must remain as her representative on our birth planet and destiny has appointed her for this role.

A moral and most admirable position, I concede. One I have done my utmost to subvert. Including recruiting the ultimate ally, Mother—she being no more eager to lose a daughter than I am to lose the sister closest to me, my daily companion.

Taking Isis's hands in hers, Mother scolded her: "Phosh. There is no reason for you to remain. You are not needed here." She then issued her most potent declaration: "All my girls can manage."

Gazing into Mother's emerald eyes, Isis stated simply, "I must remain."

Against my sister's immovable conscience and sense of duty, if even an irresistible force like Mother could not prevail, that was the end of it, except for the pain of this loss that I can no more describe than convey the sensation of having my heart ripped out of me.

But then I have never had much aptitude for description, for any sort of eloquence, having performed these official recording duties out of necessity when my sister, Minerva the historian, departed with our Unity for the stars. During our time in Sappho Valley, I fulfilled the function with minimal efficiency, but in the year and a half since members of our Unity, including Minerva, returned to Earth during the climactic time of Theo Zedera, I did my duty grudgingly and only because Minerva contended that I must do so, that she lacked continuity of presence on the planet to take it over. During the nearly four months we will be in space, I will reclaim, indeed seize in my grateful embrace my previous occupation of philosopher, its rigors and luxuries of contemplation. Minerva, historian by profession, official recorder of the history on Maternas, will henceforth chronicle our future.

A future where the most basic unknown is time itself. My sisters who journeyed here from Maternas traversed a time warp, one we must also confront on the way back. Landing on Earth, they were shocked to discover that only three years had passed since their departure from Earth, while we were equally astonished that the equivalent of twenty-five of their 336-day years had elapsed on their new world. My sister Hera, our astrophysicist, is confident she can devise a course through hyperspace that will either circumvent or locate a wormhole puncturing the time warp.

If she fails, then this is the scenario as I understand it: My sisters were four months in reaching Earth, and another four will be required to return to Maternas. Additionally, they have been on Earth for two years and four months; our astronomers and physicists, led by Hera, required all this time for research based on the knowledge they had acquired in their journeys and for full remapping and reassessments of the star systems to avoid the time warp—this, combined with fitting our ship for the return trip. A total of three years, all told, will have passed by the time we reach Maternas. If Hera fails in her navigation theories, then another twenty-five years may have passed on Maternas, more or less, depending on the vagaries of the time warp.

It is only moments now until the completely refitted Connie Esperanza departs Earth. From what I hear of the unrest that had already begun to emerge on Maternas, and from the unease that has never left the faces of Megan and my sisters Hera, Venus, and Vesta, we travel toward considerable uncertainty…

I am about to decommission this recorder and keep only my personal journal.

Farewell, beloved Earth. May our Unity continue to tend you well.

I am no longer Olympia the historian. I am now Olympia the philosopher, and I go now to Maternas.

PERSONAL JOURNAL OF JOSS

The unimaginable has become my reality.

Even though it is very late into what passes for a Maternas night, I walk along a seashore under a sky of brilliant star clusters in a canopy of red and blue fluorescence. Three moons pour silver over majestic crashing waves, greater than any I have seen even during Earth's highest tides. In a world whose daytime hours are lighted by double suns, there is never full darkness when those suns set, and I find myself in a royal-blue twilight of the most ethereal beauty.

It is sixteen hours since the landing on Maternas. Too infused with wonderment to sleep, I walk here alone, still digesting today's events.

I had fantasized endlessly about the moment when Tara and I, following our revered Mother and esteemed members of the Inner Circle—her daughters Hera, Olympia, Minerva, and Vesta—would step off the *Connie Esperanza*'s shuttle craft onto the surface of Maternas and into the wonders of an alien landscape. I had dreamed of falling into the arms of the birth family I have not seen in six Earth years. Greeting and embracing old friends. Marveling over the presence of our Unity on a new world, all those familiar to me and especially those of the Unity new to me, the children born on this home in the stars. I thought I had fully anticipated the emotional upheaval I would experience, so it never occurred to me that I would be unable to record events as they happened.

When I stepped onto Maternas, were it not for the unmistakably firm ground under my feet and the nectar-like air I breathed, or the roar of greeting that vibrated in my ears, I could have been back in those disorienting months of hurtling through hyperspace. Back in the daydream in which I stand on Maternas, land of legend, amid the waist-high ivory grass I have seen only in facsimile. Instead I was frozen in place, holding scarcely a coherent thought, unable to record a single moment of my birth family struggling their way through a churn of bodies toward me; I was capable only of trembling, of weeping.

Thousands waited to welcome us, strewn in fantastical array around our landing area, a natural amphitheater created by mountains on three sides with a coral lake forming the fourth. The crowds screamed their joy in greeting those whom they had mourned for lost on the journey to Earth, and cheered their welcome to those of us venturing here for the first time.

Mother, gathering her ceremonial green robe around her, seemed disconcerted, even shaken by the bedlam, and raised both hands in that universal request to quiet the deafening affection raining down on us, a gesture that resulted only in even greater clamor at the return of this most revered personage among us. Megan, the beloved leader of the first expedition to Maternas, was met by her own wave of pandemonium, the endless chanting of her name. But she was oblivious, rushing toward the three who ran pell-mell toward her—her beloved Laurel, and their two daughters, Emerald and Crystal.

With my senses inundated, I was able to take in only a tiny fraction of what transpired, and then my birth family overwhelmed me. "Silke," I sobbed, embracing her in a bursting agony of love and gratitude, my need so imperative and childlike that I crushed the warm solidity of her against me. Hurriedly, I buried my face against her neck to conceal what I am sure was transparent: visceral shock at my first close-up sight of my birth mother.

My trauma would have been far greater had I not been forearmed for the moment—if Vesta, when the failure of our attempt to circumvent the time warp was discovered, had not immediately begun to counsel all eighty of us on board, including even Mother and the Inner Circle.

The presence on the *Connie Esperanza* of this highly gifted psychologist could not have been more vital. During the time required to traverse the Pleiades, her preparation for our landing combined group counseling with pictorial presentations of the decades of Maternas history she had requested to be sent to our ship's computers from Maternas. We in turn sent extensive reports of ourselves and the astonishing developments on planet Earth to Maternas.

To further ameliorate the stunning theft from us of the kind gradualness of time, the ship's message banks were allowed to overflow with the fondest messages of greeting to and from the planet, and a series of holographic representations of our loved ones aging throughout the years was presented in privacy to each of us.

Even so, the jolt of seeing Silke had routed all this careful preparation. My sister Trella was obviously suffering her own dislocation; she simply gaped at me. Six years ago, when I last saw her, I was her older sister; I was now the younger by more than five decades.

"Let me go, Joss," Silke ordered, and struggled within my paralyzed arms, prying me away from her. "You've grown into a grand woman," she cried, gripping my head in both hands, then cupping my face, tracing my features with her fingers. "You are so *young*!" she screeched with such delight that it caused Trella to grimace and filled me strangely with pain.

"You," I stammered, staring back at her, "you look…you look…magnificent."

And she did. Fifty-five years on this planet had added age to her in the gentlest of fashion. Her face, framed in a simple fall of fine silver-blond hair, was an elegant filigree of age, her eyes a cleaner blue than I remembered. Her skin had burnished into gold under the double suns of this world.

I turned to my sister and hugged her tightly to me and amid the frenzy that reigned around us I put my lips to her ear to declare, "It's *good* to see you. If only I can grow to look like you!" If indeed I could be anything like my supple, gracefully mature sister…

One aspect of Trella had not changed: her shyness. "We have so very much to share with each other," she told me, eyes downcast, cheeks dimpling in a smile, an achingly familiar shadow of youth in the foreign maturity of her face. Then, shaking her head as if greater awareness had just arrived, she said proudly, "Joss, meet my daughters, Nitara and Verda."

I am ashamed to say I could not take in Trella's two daughters even as they spoke graciously and embraced me. My glance had fallen upon the three virtually nude, statuesque women behind them, waiting to make their own greetings to me.

Trella continued, introducing those three, "And these are their daughters, Niabi, Kaylee, Netis."

Something in her face and in her tone seemed odd, but I was distracted by these three, each of whom extended both hands to me. Fleetingly, I noticed that all three appeared to be around my age or younger and that they wore stretch bands to hold their ample breasts, roughly made sandals on their feet—and nothing more. Their eyes held me fast. Enormous coral eyes, mesmerizing. Unlike the black pupils of everyone on Earth, theirs glowed of ivory. They were women of confident bearing, broad-shouldered, tall, fully fleshed—Netis fair-skinned, Kaylee copper, Niabi ebony—and were differently and inexpressibly beautiful. They exuded health and sexuality.

I also noticed that everyone around me seemed as hypnotized by this arresting, newest generation as I, and were staring at them—staring in a manner I found disconcerting and inexplicable: Their stares were visibly pained, wary, loving, anxious.

As I clasped hands with Netis, Kaylee, and Niabi in turn, they held my hands in theirs with evaluation in their gaze: cool measurement. I felt their distance. I felt them to be alien. Yet I also felt beguiled by them.

Breaking away from these women, I returned my attention to Nitara and Verda, who had conveyed more genuine warmth in their welcome, and who were also more conventionally Earth-like in appearance. Nitara's exquisite face held elements of an Oriental heritage; Verda was more clearly Indian. What all these descendants of Trella told me with their genetic patterns was that Trella had had each daughter with a different sexual partner, and these two daughters had followed the same paths in having their own children, and that somehow this new generation displayed altogether different genetic variations. Of course a new and free culture would have evolved on this alien world, I told myself. And it would be one far removed from my own experience of societal control and repression.

Feeling oddly adrift and disoriented, I glanced helplessly about for Tara, my closest companion before and during our journey from Earth. Although she had disembarked from the shuttle craft by my side along with Megan, her sister, she had quickly vanished under the crush of greeting. I searched the surging, celebratory crowd with faint hope, knowing she and Megan would be enfolded in the ardent embrace of their closest family members, just as I was in mine, the family who was now clamoring for me to leave this mad scene and accompany them to a place of privacy. As if she had somehow received a telepathic message of my seeking her, Tara waved from a raised platform at least one hundred women away from me. A pale-haired, gray-eyed version of Megan, she stood next to her birth family, and I was immediately comforted by this touch of the familiar.

The seven members of the Inner Circle, stately in their customary robes, had been led to this platform, well above the jostling, rowdy crowd, along with Mother, and Megan and her family—which of course included her sister, my Tara. Megan's family was fully immersed in their reunion, while the Inner Circle viewed the tumult with various expressions ranging from proud approval on the aristocratic face of Hera to the all but glassy-eyed bemusement of Olympia, like me here for the first time, and similarly unable to find an emotional foothold.

Tara. How like her sister she is in the steely grace of her strength. I do not deserve her. She has been such solace for body and soul during the past three years while I recovered from the deep wounds inflicted by my searing encounters with Theo Zedera and Africa Contrera. Those end days of Earth were more than anyone could cope with, much less someone like myself with a mere two decades of life to her name. Africa had taken up so much of my days and nights—my awareness, my music, my dreams—that to this day her face remains on the periphery of my vision, her presence in my soul.

For a year after she left I went into deep retreat, and Tara waited for me, understanding that I required reflection and time to heal, but not understanding the true depth of my grief. That I have retained Tara's love through all this travail is a gift I do not nearly merit. Because—this is my inescapable truth—to this day I still love Africa...dream of her, long for her, mourn her.

Seeing my gaze fixed in Tara's direction, Silke asked me, "Is that Tara? We must meet this woman who is so meaningful to you."

Tara had been part of the summary of news I sent from the ship. I responded gratefully, "Yes, of course you must."

As we pushed our way through the throng, I was able to

absorb more of the chaos around me. All of the youngest women I observed had those unsettling, ethereal coral eyes. Also, the younger the female, seemingly the less she wore, all of the youngest a mere band to hold their breasts. Older generations wore clothing, flowing trouser suits of synsilk, or pants and shirts.

I also noticed it was the older generation that appeared overjoyed at this reunion of our Sisterhood. The youngest women appeared strangely detached, aloof, even dispassionate. And were already beginning to drift away.

When we reached the platform, Megan, in the shirt and pants and high boots in the black and white colors customary to her as leader of the expedition to this world, stood on the platform waving to the chanting crowd, arm in arm with Laurel, a motherly woman with cascades of gray hair and visible, palpable warmth; she seemed close to bursting with her happiness at Megan's return. I stared at the crystal she wore around her neck: I had learned that at Laurel's joining ceremony with Megan, Megan had given her this crystal, the very first object she had picked up after the landing on Maternas. Megan seemed stunned by the uproar of greeting and the family whose faces she endlessly searched as if seeking immediate clues to the events she had missed in their lives during the past twenty-five years.

Bestowing an enthusiastic embrace upon me, Laurel said, "Tara has told us *all* about you."

I could only wonder what "all" consisted of as I introduced my birth family to Tara, and Laurel presented me to her children, Emerald and Crystal. Then to their daughters, Quira and Taura.

This time it was not the newest members of Tara's family I found hypnotic—I was only vaguely mindful of Quira and Taura. Or indeed of Crystal.

I had certainly become fixated on the eyes of the women on this planet, but the eyes of this woman…I had seen that particular hue before, of course, in the eyes of Mother and Megan, the only members of the Unity to possess it until the birth of this woman, Megan's first child. Clad in a dazzling full-sleeved white shirt and white pants, she moved with casual grace toward me, and I was taken irresistibly back into the mythology of my childhood of white-winged, white-robed beings. This angel—tall, dark-haired, vanishingly slender—gazed at me out of those rectangular emerald eyes in a sun-bronzed face of fine bones, framed by dark hair cropped in feather-like, tousled strands. Her hands were slim and cool in mine, with long fingers. I could not hear her soft voice in the cacophony around us, but her lips shaped the words: "Welcome, Joss."

Megan was fixated on her as well—this daughter who had been a child of only eight years when Megan left for Earth. Emerald had been restless, adventurous, captivating, Megan told us during one of the endless days in space when we spoke of those closest to us. She had become a captivating woman.

My fascination extended well beyond her physicality. I immediately saw that the spectacular eyes that so briefly rested on me were far, far older than a mere thirty-eight years. I had known firsthand eyes like hers; I recognized the knowingness, the deep intelligence infused with pain, the despairing wisdom. I knew this woman bore a burden that haunted her. I knew it because of Africa.

My immediate impulse was to take her by the shoulders and tell her, *You don't know what suffering is. No one has ever carried burdens like Africa. Whatever your pain, it is but a feather compared to the crushing responsibility, the blame Africa took upon herself: the subjugation and death of millions.*

I was being grossly unfair, I quickly conceded. Emerald knew nothing of Africa; they could not be more dissimilar. Yet somehow, Emerald was her spiritual personification. How did I know it? I could not fathom how. I simply did. To the very marrow of my bones.

Tara took my arm, a bit forcefully. Aware that I was staring, I forced my attention away, assembled a smile, took Tara's hand, and concentrated my energies on the obligations of courtesy. I turned to greet the members of the Inner Circle, only to see esteemed Venus, arms crossed over her ample breasts, inspecting me in the frankest possible manner, her gaze drifting from my breasts to my thighs and then back. This despite the fact that I stood hand-in-hand with Tara, and Venus herself was accompanied by a most comely young woman who appeared besotted with her to the point of intoxication. Venus, the most voluptuous of Mother's daughters, had won a reputation in the realm of the sexual act that had become legendary on two planets, and it had clearly not diminished with age: I could not prevent myself from feeling her magnetic pull. My nipples tightened, and a flush spread from my face to surge hotly over my body.

"Venus," Minerva said tartly, "I see that at least one thing has not changed since our departure."

Venus tossed her mane of silver hair. "Minerva," she retorted, "now you're so much younger than I—and what a waste. I would be using the years to far greater benefit."

"To whom? Quality has always been my preference," Minerva said mildly, glancing over at her longtime companion, Christa, who was in conversation with Hera. "I enjoy having something occupy my mind besides my next carnal pleasure."

Venus looked at her with something close to pity in her azure eyes. "I have good years left," she murmured, smiling and again boldly surveying me before she strolled away, sliding an arm around her companion, her blue robe swirling around her curvaceous body.

I had had limited sexual experience, and truthfully, the vast experience and expertise of Venus were not only intimidating but unimaginable. Gazing at her bewitched companion, I wondered what would it be like to surrender myself to a woman like Venus. Again I flushed, this time to the roots of my hair, because I realized that Mother, arms folded, had been observing me. In amusement.

Mother said to Diana, "Has Venus managed to seduce every woman on this planet?"

"I have not taken a census on the matter, Mother," Diana replied, and became far more serious as she continued. "Certainly, none of the younger ones have succumbed to her."

"I was forty-five when I met her father," Mother said to me. "Had I known he'd take me to so backwater a planet as Earth, I would never—"

"Yes, we're all going to Vesta's house now," Demeter said. That this gray-robed daughter of Mother's would dare interrupt her told me she had heard this story innumerable times.

"But once I had selected him," Mother continued inexorably, "he had no more choice than an insect in a Venus flytrap. My well-named daughter has inherited that particular facility from me. The difference being, I did lose all interest after a time, men being such a bore."

The actual difference being that women are never boring, I thought. Perhaps Venus had loved someone early in her life and would never again offer deep commitment and risk suffering further loss. Perhaps, after my hopeless love for Africa, cherishing many women instead of loving just one might be my own best course.

I did not dare look at Tara as this subversive thought coursed through me. I did, however, steal the briefest of glances at Emerald who stood, hands on her hips, watching the sea of women surrounding our platform as if she had never before seen such a sight. Perhaps she hadn't. There was so much I did not know about this planet...

"We will have refreshments," Demeter said firmly. "Then—"

"My dear one, I've had quite enough of festivities," Mother said, gathering her robe around her. "I wish to return to my house."

"Something else has not changed," Vesta murmured to Minerva. "Mother's aversion to socializing."

But Mother appeared distressed by something Demeter had leaned over to say to her. "When did this happen?" she demanded.

"Four years ago. Seismic activity has increased in our area of Femina over the last two decades—"

Diana interrupted. "Erika will explain."

Mother waved a hand. "I have no interest in details, especially the gibberish of a geophysicist."

"You will be interested in these details," Diana said darkly.

Demeter continued as if never interrupted, "Our choices were abandoning this location or redesigning our dwellings. We put it to a vote and chose redesign."

Mother nodded. "As would I. This is one of the loveliest places on the planet. Am I to live in a tent, then?"

The Inner Circle laughed merrily at this absurdity, and so did I.

"My whoofie," Mother suddenly said. "When did my whoofie—"

"Nineteen years ago," Diana replied, her dark eyes sad. "He was special to all of us. He is interred with us, his ashes combined with those of our own dead in Nepenthe."

Mother nodded sadly.

I knew about this pet of mother's that she had adopted her first day on Maternas; I had seen many reproductions of these enchanting creatures. Half a meter in height, with large dark eyes and soft fur, they seemed a cross between two extinct Earth species, a koala and a marmoset.

"There are many more about," Diana offered.

Mother waved a hand and said disconsolately, "Your poor old mother will need time to take in all the changes. I'm tired, I wish now to go to my abode, whatever it is."

Now, as I walk along this seashore I am suddenly as weary as Mother—and for much the same reason. For her, in the few Earth years she has been away from a world that had become her home, everything has unexpectedly changed. As for me, even though I did live for a time in strange circumstances, I am in a world far more alien than anything I could have prepared for. And I am overcome by all that has transpired.

PERSONAL JOURNAL OF MINERVA

The balconies and bridges of Cybele surge with joyous women; the town square churns with energy. Cybele thrums with drums and throbs with melody, many in our Unity dancing in abandon. Food is everywhere; breads, cheeses, fruit in beautiful presentation on broad serving leaves, presented on tables along with other delicacies, some of which I cannot identify, and wine.

Yet I am in disarray over the transformation of this world I once knew so well. Not only the changes in those inhabiting it but also in the world itself.

I have the duty to present calmness to Christa and our daughter Celeste who depend on me for wisdom and perspective, and I have done my best by them. But I suffer such disorientation that only now, here in Cybele, deep in the evening of our return to Maternas, am I able to find a quiet place and take refuge in my profession and actually record these events.

I begin this narrative only now, having made no effort to record the anguish of our departure from Earth nor the lonely drifting days of our journey. Historian I may be, but I am impoverished as a rock when describing emotion, including—perhaps especially—my own. My sisters' journals will convey far better than any report of mine their desolation at leaving Earth; and unique talents like Astrea and Joss have already interpreted in their poetry and music the end of our three-year sojourn and journey back to Maternas.

None of us was unsettled in her decision to leave. We were fully committed, body and soul. Nonetheless, it was wrenching for us to leave Earth, perhaps more so for those like myself who were departing her magnificent shores a second time.

Not quite six years ago in Terran time, we fled an Earth of oppression, a place inimical to us. This time Earth was in all ways at peace and while she may never be restored to her pre-technology, prewar blue-green Gaia of legend, she was indeed healing, and all women who cherish her have combined their female energies in promoting that healing.

When the *Connie Esperanza*—so named for the heroic pioneer whose discovery of Estrova gave us ultimate reproductive freedom and biological independence from men—fired up her engines to disengage from Earth, I was already sorely afflicted by homesickness. There was no question that my body and my heart resided on this lovely coral world of Maternas, but a large part of my soul will always belong to the azure skies and majestic seas of Earth. Even Mother, accorded the privilege of boarding last, when the noisy bustle was over and all of us were in place, made her farewells early and was instead first on board, in seclusion in her quarters, and remained there for much of the eighteen days to the Einsteinian Curve where the catapult into hyperspace would take us beyond all contact with Earth.

I have not begun this history until now for good reason. The close quarters during our journey on the *Connie Esperanza,* the lack of privacy, the quarrels and ill tempers among us—it was all too much the same as it was on the previous trips to and from Maternas, tiresome and predictable. I suppose I have grown querulous with age, but why would I record its unbecoming and petty details all over again?

We had just broken out of hyperspace, drifting within the spectacular red-blue hues of the Pleiades, when we achieved contact with Maternas. With no means of communicating with them while we were in hyperspace or on Earth, and given the time lapse, our Unity on Maternas had long since assumed the worst: that we were lost in space. Celebration if not bedlam reigned on Maternas.

Not so for us. The dismay on board our ship was palpable. Hera's face resembled a cosmic storm. Despite the originality—the brilliance—of her theories and the soundness of our scientific computations, navigating the bore hole through the time warp failed; it apparently closed as we reached it, or perhaps our reaching it caused it to close.

We were faced with the immutable reality that during the nearly three Earth years since we left, thirty more years—not twenty-five, as before—had elapsed on Maternas. An eternity. Surely incomprehensible. I understand the paradox of a time warp but still cannot put my mind around the stunning actuality that so much time has passed on a planet we left a seemingly scant few years ago.

I must count myself among the very fortunate, those whose closest loved ones accompanied them on the voyage to Earth; Christa and our daughter Celeste were with me.

Celeste is prostrate over the reality that her friends, her entire peer group, are suddenly three decades older than she. But I can scarcely conceal my relief. I cannot imagine the grief of losing all those years of witnessing Celeste's life had she not been with us…

Megan is among the not so fortunate. Laurel, and their daughters Emerald and Crystal, are thirty years older than when Megan left Maternas on what we had all believed to be no more than a year's voyage to visit our sisters on Earth to bring news of the home we had found in the stars, and then return. Megan is conducting herself as the leader she is, but I recognize how dazed and distraught she feels.

As for those journeying to Maternas for the first time, such as Megan's sister, Tara, and her companion, young Joss, their dislocation is even more severe: For them, fifty-five Maternas years have gone by; all those they know on the planet will have passed them by in every manner of life experience.

When we descended from orbit, our planet looked in every way the same. Yet all has changed.

I am Minerva the historian, and while others have assumed the official duties of the chronicle of our Unity on Maternas, it is under these astounding, unprecedented circumstances that I have resumed my own personal journal of what transpires from here.

If there is a complexity of emotion about my return, I do feel a simple and pure joy to be reunited with my sisters. Whatever has happened, our Unity is still a society entirely of our own making, our habitation is wholly of our own design. And although I am too far emotional to have any appetite for food, the celebration is like those we held for our major anniversaries of the landing here. The graceful carved utensils are identical to those we created when we first came to Maternas, and the smells of the foods of this world could not be more comforting if I were a child again being nourished by Mother.

Odd to say that the nocturnals are another comfort. These violent winds have always circumscribed our lives by forcing us indoors for several hours each evening, an imperative we have no choice but to heed—no act of ours can prevent or diminish their screaming rise each evening. As the sudden coolness at sunset collides with the warmth of the sun-drenched land, the bora-type winds arrive each evening and scour our land. The trees are like the palms on Earth in a hurricane, bending horizontal, their branches and long leaves flowing with the wind. Vegetation is deeply rooted, with shrubbery of intricate branch-work, acclimatized and well suited to withstanding wind—unlike we puny, fragile humans who flee to protect ourselves behind our rock walls. Over the years I became accustomed to the nightly familiarity of nocturnals, and I've missed the music from the flute-like carvings Zandra sculpted into our homes, the erratic patterns of the winds playing haunting notes on these carvings. This evanescent music never ceases to be eerily compelling, and in some measure transmutes and tames the winds' power and ferocity.

Our musicians produce their own more mellow beauty: hypnotically sweet strains that Kiva, Nishi, and Kistna induce from two crystal flutes and air percussion. I am actually surprised by this music, as is Celeste. Thirty years having passed—where are our younger musicians? Where is the appalling music one would expect from a younger generation out to shock and displease its elders? Such rebellious behavior has occurred from time immemorial…

Little has changed here concerning food, but tastes and dishes evolve gradually, perhaps even more so on a world where reverence is paid to all living entities, where utmost care is taken for ecology. But human behavior is a different matter, and throughout history each generation challenges whatever structure is in place as part of its breaking away into what psychologist Vesta calls individuation.

Individuation is clearly present in our youngest women, and it could not be more extreme or unsettling. Of the thousands who have converged on Cybele's main square for the night's celebration, none are of that youngest generation. Those born to the four thousand who first arrived are here as are their daughters, but as for the next generation of descendants not one attends the fete celebrating our return. Venus has just confirmed this fact for me: not one. I am shocked; she is not. "Typical," she says resignedly. But apparently not entirely typical.

Which brings me to the strangest occurrence of all:

where these youngest women have taken themselves. Mother is not with us in Cybele's main square; she rests in Demeter's house; and many of the newest generation are gathered outside that house. Thousands in number. They assembled after the nocturnals receded, ringing the house in rows extending far up into the encircling hills, well beyond where the eye can see. They hold hands; they stand in silence, apparently in homage to Mother. It is an amazing sight, its strangeness indescribable. I can only imagine how unnerved Mother must feel, especially, according to Demeter, after she ventured outside the house and went to the first row of arm-linked young women.

"Shoo," she said with sweeps of her hands as if to disperse a flock of pigeons. "Tell everyone I don't want—" But the group's instant response was to sink to its knees before her, bending their foreheads toward the coral-hued earth, whereupon Mother turned and fled back into the house.

I comfort myself that I am together with my birth sisters on this planet for the very first time—except of course for Selene, who died many years ago in the Antarctic on Earth, and for Isis who took it upon herself to remain on Earth. Though all of us were born within minutes of each other, we are so different now. Because of the time warp, Diana, Demeter, and Venus are shockingly older than Vesta, Olympia, Hera, and me—by thirty years. Olympia, having been among those remaining on Earth, is fifty-five years younger, a time difference with which she is grappling. And she is changed in a different way, quieter, more introspective, changed by the events she was part of with our Unity on Earth.

And yet…and yet underneath all external appearances we are still not all that different. Diminutive Vesta is the dear person she always was, the sweetest of any of us. Hera, the tallest of us, is her polar opposite in every other way, no less forthright and arrogant today than when we were children together. Demeter and Diana, with their even temperaments and their practicality, have always occupied the middle ground between the extremes in our original nine. Olympia, as self-effacing as ever, still is not able to see—or perhaps believe—the extent of her own gifts. Venus—well, what more is there to say about Venus? Even now she casts savoring glances over the women around her—as she apparently has every single day of her life. For many women even half her age, such behavior would win ridicule. But not Venus. Women are made shy by her interest, even preen under her gaze, and fall willingly under her sway, accepting the limited duration of her attention as if fully conceding to her the nature of a bee supping nectar from a garden of blossoms. I have never understood it. But then I am her sister, not a conquest. I am the kind of woman whose heart insists upon leading her body.

She is right to boast that she has many good years left. Life expectancy continues to expand, and this planet, with its 336-day year and its lighter-than-Earth gravity, its slightly enriched oxygen content, is kind to its inhabitants, the moderate climate on our continent of Femina adding to the equation.

But what of that generation gathered in such solemnity outside Demeter's house? They are all so young, many of them barely past toddler stage. All of them, whatever their age, stand in silence along the hills of Cybele, and that utter silence troubles me greatly, is more eerie than I can describe…

Even more eerie, even more troubling is what Diana has just told me: They never speak. Ever.

PERSONAL JOURNAL OF JOSS

It is sunrise in this alien land, the radiance of its double suns making vision hurtful, despite anything I do with ocular modifications. Part of my discomfort may be my aversion to food since we arrived, and that I have not slept; each time my eyelids drifted closed during the night, my head spun sickeningly, as if from overindulgence in an intoxicant.

Even though I was given warnings as part of our departure preparations that I might suffer this symptom of sensory disorientation, I had discounted them. After all, I had already ventured to what I had considered alien terrain at the far ends of the Earth—the Arctic and the Antarctic poles—and into the subterranean world of Sappho Valley. No warning, no amount of guidance could have prepared me for this aching sense of separation from the planet I have always known; and like someone constantly attempting to use an amputated limb, I cannot prevent myself from seeking what I have always assumed was there. I expect to see blue skies, blue-green seas, green trees, and foliage, and I am jarred by these coral seas and ivory-blue landscapes. Never again will I experience darkness at night, only an endless twilight.

Hoping to adjust soon to these unalterable circumstances, I force my thoughts away from my surroundings, for safety if not sanity. Where my thoughts alight is perhaps not entirely safe, but it is firmer ground to be sure.

I think of Emerald. Focus on my memories of her from last evening. Vivid memories...yesterday and during the evening I could no more prevent my gaze from returning to her than if a work of fine art were within my sight.

She moves like a dancer. Or perhaps more like a runner, since her movements have that tight economy seen in superb athletes. She is the embodiment of her mother, Megan, whom I have had the pleasure to observe closely over the many months of her sojourn on Earth and our time in space. Like Megan, Emerald stands balanced lightly on the balls of her feet in what seems readiness for flight, with her head cocked slightly to one side as if in a stillness of absorbed listening, arms by her side or crossed over her chest. Another signature habit reminiscent of Megan is brushing hair from her forehead, although Emerald's hair is more orderly and her fingers are paler, almost translucent in their slenderness, and her hair falls into new patterns of dark glossiness with the passage of her fingers, patterns so lovely I found myself constantly glancing at her in hopes she would repeat this act.

A deeper commonality she shares with Megan: an essential loneliness. Seeing this quality always in Africa, I recognize that it often is a by-product of the responsibilities of leadership. But unlike Mother, the grand leader of us all, who intimidates everyone save the daughters born directly to her, Megan as a leader is approachable and held in the highest affection as well as the greatest esteem by the women of this planet. Emerald is much more in Mother's mold.

I noticed that women here seemed more than aware of Emerald, their gazes lingering longer than what would be considered idle interest. Yet their attention moved away, and even when Emerald happened to catch their eyes with an intersecting glance, the women would merely nod and not approach. In watching her over the course of the evening, I gained two sure impressions: that I was one of many who found her an object of beauty and fascination; and that while her elation at the return of Megan was evident, unlike her sister Crystal, who constantly embraced her birth mothers in an excess of jubilation, the welcoming ceremonies had become a tedium to Emerald, and only her sense of obligation to Megan kept her there.

Could these sisters be more dissimilar? Crystal—blond, blue-eyed, full-figured, vivacious; while Emerald—slender, intense, quiet, withdrawn—is the shadow to her sun. I was not alone in my absorption in these two sisters; Megan stared at her daughters, continually touched and briefly embraced them as if needing to reaffirm their very existence. Yet the expression in her eyes was quizzical and perturbed, and edged with grief. This latter emotion I well understood, given my own lurching bewilderment whenever I gazed at Silke and Trella, having to bridge the gap of years with my own family. At one point Megan came to me and silently circled me with an arm. No words were necessary between us. We shared the same anguish at the years we had both suddenly lost, for her the years of watching two children blossom into women, the years of watching her lover Laurel age into the woman of grace and dignity she has become. My family too had moved into an orbit outside my own life. I did not want to go to whatever place they wished to take me; I wanted to find somewhere dark and quiet, to hide there until I could begin to digest some of what I had seen.

Tara, also overcome by the sudden changes wrought by the bending of time, paid me scant attention now that I had found her; she hovered close to Megan, an ineffectual buffer between Megan and the adoring women whose leader she had been during the perilous first journey into the stars. Her willingness to accommodate their greeting and expressions of affection was admirable, but the crush of women wishing to speak to her, touch her, express joy and relief at her return, was never-ending and more than I could have possibly borne.

It was under these circumstances that my first substantive contact with Emerald occurred. I had been gazing at her yet again, and to my discomfiture she not only looked up to meet my eyes but walked over, to chide me, I was certain, for my staring at her. "This situation for my mothers," she said, leaning close to me to be heard in the tumult. "It's out of control. Perhaps we should—"

"Enlist Tara and Crystal and form ourselves into a barricade," I said, recovering my wits and assessing the area before she could voice her next words. My close contact with Africa Contrera, the finest synthesist of information Earth had ever produced, had not been entirely wasted on me. "And from there open a path."

Emerald nodded. "It cannot look obvious. My mothers will not put themselves above anyone in the Unity." With a sudden and altogether charming grin, she added, "They'd rather be trampled."

We implemented the plan well, unobtrusively recruiting Crystal, Laurel, and a woman named Danya who had herself been ineffectually attempting to safeguard Megan. Forming a phalanx of interceptors under the guise of making our own greetings, we engaged with each woman to briefly explain that there were limitless tomorrows and for the sake of Megan's emotional state they should confine themselves to a brief greeting. Laurel did her part by assuring longtime friends of Megan that she would soon organize opportunities when they would have many private visits with her.

It was while we were performing this task that I said to Emerald, "The youngest among you. How odd that none are here. They—"

She turned on me.

"They seem…un, un…uh, unusual."

There was such cold, forbidding distance in her green eyes that the final word had come stuttering out of me.

She said quietly, "You have a great deal to learn about our world."

PERSONAL JOURNAL OF OLYMPIA

Irony of all ironies. That phrase passes through my mind constantly. It so aptly sums up the current situation.

From everything previously said to me on Earth by Mother and my other sisters, from all I had viewed and studied of information provided by the computers of our ship, I had expected to find Maternas a lovely, idyllic world. In its purely physical sense, it is—beyond anything I expected. This world's glory is so without compare that I cannot fathom how any member of the Unity managed to tear herself away for the return visit to Earth.

The air on Maternas is a sensuous delight, a sweet soft caress, perfumed by flowers and grasses and soil warmed into rich aromas by our double suns. When I first stepped onto the surface, only my years and the dignity I am bound to maintain as a member of the Inner Circle prevented me from dancing, from joining the company of the more scantily garbed.

Constrained though I am in my conventional robe, I savor the constant sweet thrumming of insects blending with the calls of creatures peacefully sharing this world, the humming breezes of daytime. I am enchanted by the coral and ivory-blue colors of the landscape, our night skies of fiery grandeur, and even the nocturnal winds that scream through our settlement each evening like some tireless ghost of a twentieth-century train.

Cybele, the Unity's habitat on this world, is a wonder. An extension of the natural order, not born of a process of demolishing and recreation, homes are sculpted from the hills, with only their interior rooms private, their main entrance open to land and sky and any visitor, human or animal. We all carry devices that emit a current of variable strength to protect ourselves against any large animal that may wander in, but virtually all are welcome, especially whoofies, which overrun the settlement—no surprise. Quadruped primates about a foot in height, with soft dark fur and huge dark eyes, they are endearingly clumsy, their whoofs for food and affection irresistible, and everyone feeds and loves them.

Other buildings and structures have been built as necessary and without depredation of the landscape, from stores of naturally occurring rock and stone in the planet's mantle. Exteriors of the homes are formed by the angular, weathered grays and brown of the hills that enfold them, but the interiors are curving interconnected rooms enhanced by the colors of illumination particles added to the obsidian and igneous rock, and floor and wall coverings of fleece and tapestries.

Of my sisters, Venus lives in Cybele, desiring "to take in the passing scene," she tells me, one of her many euphemisms for pursuing her romantic adventures. Demeter also lives there, a necessity in her practice of the medical arts. Vesta and Carina reside along the Toklas River not far from Diana, who chose a home in the tiny artists colony on the shore of Stein Lake. Minerva's house, where I am staying for now, is a small dwelling of peaceful grays and gray-blues beside the Woolf River.

Mother's home was high on Cybele's main hill, overlooking Radclyffe Falls and Vivien Lake. I say *was* because a series of severe temblors that struck during her absence on Earth revealed the dangers of its location. She is presently staying with Demeter until a new home is fashioned according to her preferences.

Geological prediction on Earth, while nowhere near an exact science, plots probabilities with relatively high accuracy—within weeks. I was surprised by the comments of Erika, a renowned geoscientist—who looks like one with masses of unruly auburn hair around a thin, scholarly face—when she elaborated: "It's different here from Earth, and Femina has proven to be different from other continents on Maternas. Earthquake intensity doesn't correlate to any traditional measurement of subterranean magma flow or the motions of continental plates. It's an anomaly we don't as yet understand."

One anomaly among many. Such as large waterspouts created by the speed of the planet's daily revolution that whirl in off the ocean to suddenly drench us even in bright sunshine. The colony appears indifferent to the inconvenience, and I myself find it another delightful sensual experience—a warm deluge somewhat like standing briefly in a waterfall. Most of us walk barefoot, especially when near the ocean in the exquisite seaside moss, and our clothes—trouser suits and belted tunics—are impervious to drenchings.

Femina is not without its negative aspects. Each spring brings an influx of parasitic spores borne by the winds, and as the newest arrivals we immediately received an infusion of antibodies to begin immunization against these lethal organisms. Also, unaccountably, a higher percentage of us than on Earth choose to end our lives, and many fall sway to phobias. Despite the best efforts of our psychologists, some wander off into the mountains, never to be seen again…

And there is that largest negative. Most of our Unity fled Earth in the belief that gross abuse of nationalistic power had ushered in an ever darkening age with no hope for any end to its repression. When I departed, after the brief and shocking series of events in which our Unity played the major role, Earth was suddenly and universally at peace, its newly freed populace witnessing the dawning of a new age, a radical departure from its blood-soaked past. I now find myself on a world where not only have fifty-five years elapsed in contrast to the six that have passed for me, but an entire generation is in rebellion against a status quo of freedom and self-determination. Theirs is in no manner an Earth-like rebellion of violent, bloody revolution, but one of a nature that will be made clearer to me soon, when our Inner Circle gathers at the Council Chambers in Cybele.

Despite all that confronts us, I am enormously excited to be on this new world. When I left Earth, it had been long bereft of the woman I cherish above all others. This precious, tender woman had chosen to be with me until she could no longer bear the unrelenting visibility of being partnered with a member of the Inner Circle. She chose to go to Maternas with Nerisa, and this was a prime reason I remained on Earth. While I was on the platform during the welcoming festivities, I heard a voice behind me: "My dear Olympia."

"My Ceeley," I whispered, as I used to whisper it when we loved.

By the time I turned she was gone, vanished into the crowd.

But she is here, fifty-five years older than when we parted, and for me it is as if no time had elapsed. Did I imagine I heard love in her words, in her voice?

PERSONAL JOURNAL OF JOSS

After I provided assistance in easing the commotion around Megan in the celebration of her return, after we had returned Megan and Laurel to the quiet of their home late last night, Emerald took me aside to ask how she could repay me for my service.

"It was hardly a service," I replied. "I was happy to be of help."

A touch of impishness in her slight smile, she countered, "You might as well begin learning our methods of exchange. All of us are indebted to one another in many ways for services rendered. We strive constantly to reduce those debts."

"A unique barter system," I remarked, smiling back at her. It would be an interesting challenge to find all the ways I could be of service on this world, aside from offering my music. Remembering that Tara would be involved in consultations with the Inner Circle and Megan in these first days after our landing, and that I would be on my own, I told her, "I would like to see something of my new world. Could you assist me with that?"

The slow, pleased smile that emerged from the austere beauty of her face was perhaps the loveliest I have ever seen.

Thus we fly above Maternas on the *Sarah Bernhardt* in one

of the solar-powered craft designed for swiftness of transport and for exploration versatility. Emerald's agreement to show me my new world will far exceed any debt of hers to me, a circumstance I welcome, trusting that it will give me further opportunities to avail myself of her intriguing presence while I balance the scale.

An added benefit is that soaring above the surface of my new home has somewhat lifted the disorientation I've felt since the landing, the view from on high restoring perspective. I hope it will soon also restore my appetite, and have a lasting effect on my physical transition because I must begin my emotional one. My birth family and I have many years we need to bridge.

This excursion should hold few if any surprises: I pored over many depictions of the world of Maternas during the months in space. But while those detailed, highly comprehensive pictorials were of consuming interest, they were insufficient. However vividly presented in omnidimensional holograph, no representation can substitute for reality and a person's own choices as to what to look at and for how long, when the pleasures and impressions become purely individual.

We begin with a high east-west orbital survey of Maternas—a vista of the utmost grandeur on a day when few clouds obscure our view. Glorious coral seas surround seven ivory-blue continents on a world slightly smaller than Earth. With a slower axis rotation, its solar day takes thirty-two minutes longer than an Earth day, but its yearly rotation around its binary suns requires only 336 days. Land masses take up only twenty-three percent of this world's surface, compared with Earth's nearly thirty percent. The two smallest continents are polar, with their pinkish ivory ice fields deep and glacial. That this is a younger world than Earth is evidenced by considerable volcanic activity, both oceanic and land, columns of steam emerging from fissures under the sea and from vast calderas on the land. All the nonpolar continents contain mountain ranges of deeply etched volcanic and granite rock, and upthrust proceeds along giant earthquake faults. Forests, iridescent ivory-blue, blanket the temperate zones near the equator. "Primarily conifer," Emerald tells me. "And of fierce beauty."

She has offered minimal commentary, focusing instead on gliding us along the most informative trajectories and allowing land and sea to speak for themselves. Although I know most of what she tells me, I am happy to hear her describe it herself.

Over the continent of Femina, Emerald eases us into lower orbit. Flatlands spread out from the mountain ranges. Grasslike vegetation and low shrubbery spring into view, blending gradually into scrub forest. Grazing herds roam far and wide below us—the most numerous appearing to be small horses, and species reminiscent of Earth's giraffes and zebras, and called by the same names, Emerald tells me. Except for purposes of scientific classification, zoologists here have not troubled to bring into common usage any different names for these Earth-like species. It is a peaceful scene extending below us, herds galloping not to flee predators but out of the sheer exhilaration and vividness of life.

"Herbivores," Emerald remarks. "We have few carnivore species, most of those crocodiles. And ourselves, of course, since our consumption of fish defines us as flesh eaters. Maternas is fifty million years younger than Earth, which places it in the rough equivalent of Earth's Eocene period—"

"Shortly after the Cretaceous," I interrupt, wanting to show that I have taken the trouble to become informed about the historical perspective of what we view. "When dinosaurs became extinct."

"Yes. Although we still have one of our own, one I can't show you. He's a lethally telepathic old fellow we leave strictly to himself."

"I've heard about GEM, your green-eyed monster," I say with a grin, "and the brilliance of your mother in averting a great tragedy."

"My mother deserves every conceivable homage accorded to her." Emerald's voice has suddenly become somber. "While she was gone I never believed anything but that she would return. Everyone claimed to agree with me. But during the incredible celebration on this world when we picked up the first signal from the *Connie Esperanza,* I learned the truth. Everyone had given them up for lost."

We fly toward the southern, equatorial sector of Femina where the majority of our Unity reside. Even from a distance it is a lovely land, with gentler if deeply etched mountains, and numerous spring-fed lakes.

"We have teeming sea life," Emerald says. "A bounty."

This continent could be one of Earth's, except for the coral and ivory-blue colors of its surface, and that its ocean has no sandy shores.

When I comment about the vegetation that extends down to and past the tide lines, Emerald explains, "If we didn't have such dense ground cover, our topsoil would be scoured away by our winds. It's rich topsoil—Femina is the most fertile of the continents. Plentiful rainfall accelerates the process of breaking down its volcanic origins. But Femina is also volatile, as you'll find out. Maternas is far less stable geologically than Earth for reasons we haven't yet determined."

What she tells me is displayed below us like a topographic map: many fault lines and much displacement, patterns of raised stitching prominent across the land.

This third largest continent is six million square miles, a million of those miles a plain where forest cover is in a rapid process of geological retreat, aided in small measure by herbivores. Great creatures similar to those from Earth's prehistory range these plains, their flanks still armored, but the absence of horns points clearly to an evolutionary path where dominance on this planet is as yet undetermined. Elephants with trunks but without tusks graze peacefully on succulent shrubs. Much smaller mammals strip berries, pods, and seeds from bushes.

Cybele, the primary settlement, sits in the southwest corner of the continent, in the foothills of volcanic mountains with rugged obsidian faces, perhaps ten thousand feet at their height. Studded with dramatic waterfalls, these foothills slope precipitously down to the sea and into a verdant valley strewn with pinkish streams feeding into sparkling coral lakes. High, waving ivory grass predominates, and the landscape is liberally dotted with low flowering shrubs of yellows and golds. Some of the trees are palmlike; many others are reminiscent of Earth's ancient Joshua trees in the way the incessant, pitiless winds have pummeled them into distinctly individual shapes. These trees are multibranched conifers—leaves would not survive—and have gathered themselves in clusters for optimum defense.

The location of Cybele becomes logical when seen from the air. The mountain range is a natural barrier to animal life and must surely assist in deflecting the harshest of the seasonal winds. The foothills not only provide a source of fresh water from runoff, but plentiful rainfall collects in numerous freshwater lakes. They also help to absorb the seismic waves from earthquake tremors. It is a beautiful locale, enhanced by its spectacular coastline.

As Emerald changes course westward, she asks, "Do you know why they named this first settlement Cybele?"

Of course I do. "She's a Greek-Roman deity, Mother of the Gods and a symbol of universal motherhood—her maternity extending to nature in all its wildness. In legend she is Mountain Mother, with her sanctuaries on mountains and in caves."

"You've informed yourself well about our world," Emerald comments.

Child's play. I do not speak the thought, not wishing to offend someone proudly presenting the splendors of her home planet. For a student of history like myself, a world with only fifty-five years of recorded history requires scant study in comparison with Earth's many centuries of savagery, especially considering the reinterpretation required from distortion of historical records due to patriarchal versions of events. My study of Maternas was thorough but swift, needing to encompass merely its geology, physics, and paleontology.

"I'm guessing your profession is one of the sciences," she says.

"Nothing close," I tell her. "My major studies were history, but I'm a musician."

Emerald smiles as if wryly amused that her guess would be so wide of the mark. "What do you play?"

"Aerophonics," I reply.

"I don't know it. Is it similar to the air percussion of our musicians?"

"A distant relative." Very distant, actually. "I create my music from air currents."

"That sounds wonderful. Will I hear you play sometime?"

"It would be my pleasure."

"Tell me about your life," Emerald says, her tone casual as she heads the craft over ocean.

She surely does not mean the mundane facts of my growing up years—they differ in little respect from those of anyone in the Unity who was born on Earth. "I don't know where to begin," I parry, truly not knowing. How could I summarize, even hope to condense, the world-changing events of the past five years and my part in them?

"I'll narrow the question. Why choose to come here now instead of on the original expedition with your birth family?"

It seems a simple question, yet for me an unduly complicated one. "It was a very hard choice. The difference was a woman I was involved with." I offer no elaboration; this hint of romantic complication will perhaps suffice to deflect her curiosity into another channel.

"You don't mean Africa Contrera?" She turns to face me full

on, her eyes lighted with interest. "You were *involved* with her?"

Shocked by this utterly unexpected ambush, I counter awkwardly, "What do you know about her?"

"What everyone knows. She was one of the most famous women in history, the most brilliant Synthesist on Earth, the most visible woman in our Unity. Everyone here was always quoting her, referring to her. She was…" She searches for a word. "Everyone was awed by her. The Earth history we downloaded after your ship broke through hyperspace told us of your role when you were captured with her during the final days with Theo Zedera." She is looking at me in consuming curiosity, having turned away from the controls of our vessel; we are well out over ocean. "Are you saying there was even more involvement?"

"No. Well, yes. It's more complicated than that," I say lamely, trying somehow to cover up this inadvertent exposure.

"You did have a relationship with her?" she asks.

"Yes. Uh, no," I amend hastily.

"It must be very complicated indeed. In my frame of reference there's a wide difference between yes and no." This said without a trace of a smile.

"I mean," I stumble, "except for Theo Zedera—he was her friend from childhood—no one had a relationship with Africa. She was…" Sadness, never far under the surface in me, breaks loose, and my voice trembles as I say, "The loneliest, most isolated woman I've ever known."

"Yes," Emerald says gently. "I could see that in every image of her."

"It was what I saw from the very first…" I break off, having real difficulty controlling my voice.

"You loved her," she says simply.

"With all my heart. And for all of my life." I voiced it. Admitted it. For the first time, to anyone. And why not say it now? Africa and everything connected with her was many light-years away. "Where are we headed?" I inquire, trying to change the topic. Still, I realize the ambiguity of my question in the context of our conversation.

"Forgive my intrusion," Emerald says. After a moment of studying my face, she turns back to her controls. "Of course you'd have difficulty talking about so exalted a woman in any intimate way with a perfect stranger."

Disarmed, I speak the truth: "It's actually easier. My feeling for her was a lifelong secret. I understood how it would be viewed, that I would receive counseling to...correct my fixation."

She does not look at me, her nod barely perceptible. "You knew to keep inviolate something that came from the best place in you."

How does she understand this so well? "Thank you," I say.

"We're headed for the equatorial continent of Amazonia," she offers in reply to the question I asked a few moments ago. Then she says, "I feel a great certainty that you brought warmth and comfort to her life."

"I hope so. It's my profoundest wish," I confess. "She's the finest woman I have ever known."

"The finest woman you will *ever* know. Deserving of your deep and abiding love."

Struck dumb by a validation I never dreamed I'd receive from anyone, I stare out at the rolling ocean below us. I never thought anyone would understand my steadfast devotion to Africa Contrera. I dare to unpeel another layer of myself: "I held her in my arms," I tell her, "and loved her. For a time, I believe I may have given her comfort."

Still, Emerald does not look at me and is quiet for some moments. Then she says, "I understand," and I feel an emanation from her, from her words, that tells me she does, and that there is something deep in her that very nearly surfaced.

PERSONAL JOURNAL OF MINERVA

"Let's begin. Now."

Hera has loudly interrupted all conversations. Sweeping her royal blue cape back from her shoulders as she paces the length of the room, she halts, crosses her arms, and opens our meeting without preamble: "For those of us who made the journey to Earth, for those arriving on Maternas for the first time, it's clear the rebellion that began before we left has advanced to the point where our every sphere of influence over the newest generation has vanished. Furthermore—"

"*Every* sphere?" I interrupt rudely and with unconcealed irritation. My egocentric sister becomes ever more tiresome with her lofty burnishing of every fact with dramatics, not to mention her taking it upon herself to preside over a meeting where others are far more qualified to do so.

"I exaggerate not one whit, Minerva," she retorts, her cape sweeping in deep folds around her as she seats herself across the table from me. "I have taken the trouble of educating myself while you've merely—"

"Hera," I cut her off, "like me, you've been gone for the past thirty Maternas years. Surely it is not your province to lecture the rest of us. Surely you exaggerate. Surely we still control some spheres—"

"We do not," Demeter interjects. "But—"

"So, Minerva," Hera says, her hawk-like features ablaze in triumph, "just listen—"

"Not to you, not when others—"

"Girls. Stop your nonsense this instant," Mother snaps, rapping the table. "You're like quarrelsome six-year-olds."

"Hera, Minerva—patience," Demeter pleads, extending a placating hand to each of us. "Minerva, you truly can't imagine what's happened in your absence."

Sitting between Hera and myself, Demeter is being fair and judicious; but her usually serene features look unduly troubled. It is she who should be conducting this meeting. But from childhood my imperious sister Hera seemingly took seriously Mother's whimsical naming of us after the goddesses worshiped by the Romans and ancient Greeks, and to this day she cannot step away from her exalted opinion of herself or discuss a topic without seeming to deliver pronouncements from Mount Olympus.

Tensions run high in this room, extending beyond the friction between myself and Hera. Mother, Megan, all of us in the Inner Circle: Demeter, Diana, Vesta, Venus, Hera—and Olympia for the first time ever—are assembled around the crystal table in Cybele's council chambers to assess the crisis facing our Unity. Tara also is here by virtue of her position as leader of our Unity on Earth. That burly Danya, sitting next to me, also has been included is a further ominous portent. Though her function has always been nebulously defined in a society whose credo is nonviolence, she is in effect our senior security adviser for any matter related to the safety and protection of our Unity.

During the history of our presence on this planet, we have gathered often in this room. After we first built our homes, we came here to debate over the course of many contentious meetings the minimal governmental structure acceptable to an unconstrained yet cohering society. Fifteen years after we landed, we met here when Megan called an emergency meeting to announce that an Earth ship in our sector was sending out a distress call, and then there were the ensuing gatherings to determine the fate of that ship and its mostly male crew. Five years after that, we met here again when our plans commenced for the return journey to Earth.

Our convening today is for information gathering only and is deemed unofficial. Therefore, it is being only recorded, not transmitted to all other members of our Unity, as required by the provisions of our charter. And a good thing because we would engender little confidence from any onlooker seeking wisdom from such quarrelsome village elders. Mother projects her usual serenity, but she holds her tiny self erect with obvious effort and has made a joking reference to "jet lag," one of the quaint twentieth-century expressions she has made a hobby of invoking. Vesta and myself are also tired, stemming from our emotion-laden arrival and our struggle to adjust to the drastically changed world to which we have returned. Truthfully, Mother and my sisters and I are now of an age where weariness overtakes us more easily, and change, much less unanticipated change, can be a vexation.

While readily conceding my ignorance of the matter at hand, I do not and will not accept that Hera has appointed herself official spokesperson. I address my question to Demeter and Diana and Venus: "Are you seriously stating that our youngest women will accept no instruction or advice or guidance whatever from us?"

"The very youngest ones do not overtly reject it," Demeter tells me. "But if we insist they take part in the activities designed to educate or enlighten them, they can become inattentive or passively resistant, to the extent of displaying a kind of bored stupor, or worse, actually falling asleep."

"Surely not all of them behave like this?"

"All of them."

"Without exception?"

"All of them, Minerva." Mixed with the impatience in Demeter's voice is a quiet despair. "The older ones make no acknowledgment of us whatever."

"Diana, you told me they never speak—"

"They do speak. Until about the age of two. Then they withdraw more and more. And finally leave..."

I turn helplessly to Megan. But she sits beside Mother silent and tense, uninvolved, staring off into the distance.

Megan, generations apart from Mother, is held as close in Mother's affections as any of us in the Inner Circle. These days we all seem to have become smaller with age, and Megan is slimmer than ever in her black pants and white shirt, her dark hair handsomely limned with silver. Mother seems an even tinier figure in her green robe, her cantaloupe-size breasts just clearing the surface of the table; but those huge green eyes do not miss a nuance, including the fact that Megan sits like someone frozen in place. Undoubtedly she is, as she contemplates the strange path chosen by the newest children of her own direct descendants—and that it may be beyond even her great leadership capabilities to alter what has occurred.

As for myself, my heart palpitates with alarm. When my daughter, Celeste, agreed to accompany Christa and me to Earth, we were overjoyed. Celeste had just begun to display symptoms of a particularly willful rebellion sweeping her generation, a rebellion centered most grievously on a refusal to take part any longer in one of our more cherished traditions, the ceremonies and games surrounding the anniversary of our arrival here. We were happy to remove her from this world until calmness and perspective prevailed. Neither has occurred; rebellion has only accelerated. And Celeste is in deepest distress over her isolation—at the time warp that has suddenly placed her own generation at a three-decade remove from her. She has expressed her apprehension over what might befall any children of her own.

"What is *happening* here?" she tearfully begged me this morning. "I need to know! I need you to tell me the truth!"

It is my duty and obligation to deliver that truth to my daughter, and I address my question to Diana, our geneticist, who gazes at the table, grimness inhabiting her thin, intense face. I use great care in my phrasing: "Perhaps a genetic mutation—"

"Minerva," she erupts in instant exasperation, "could anything be more obvious? More crucial than knowing what effect living in the environment of this planet under these alien suns has had on our genetic structure? We've been performing intensive genetic analysis from the moment we first landed—as you very well know. In the time you've been gone," she continues hotly, "we've never once stopped, we've—"

"Diana." I hold both hands up, palms out. "I don't doubt that. But the physical changes are unmistakable. Their eyes—"

"Of course there would be changes," Hera snorts. "No planet in the cosmos could possibly be an exact duplicate of Earth."

As I suck in breath to pour a flame of sarcasm over my maddening sister, Demeter again places a restraining hand on my sleeve, and biologist Venus says softly, "We are convinced beyond any shadow of any doubt that all outward physical changes in the youngest members of our Unity are environmentally based. Considering the gestation periods of our pregnancies average no more than five or six months, and that we have been fifty-five years consuming the bounty of our planet, and its water, the predominant coral and ivory pigment molecules of Maternas have finally superimposed themselves over the green-based chlorophyll of Earth."

I cannot help gazing at the water in the vessels from which each of us sips, then at the great platter of fruit on the table, at the delicious berry compote created for us by Vesta…

"In plain language," Mother says, "you're saying that our offspring are assimilating into an alien landscape."

"Correct," Venus says with a lightening of expression on her sensuous face that might pass for a faint smile. "In addition to the changes in eye coloration, some sexual change is evident—more and more enhancement in the clitoral area. Making the act even more pleasurable for the newer generations," she says with more than a touch of wistfulness. "Understandable, of course. Female freedom on Maternas has given women more sexual liberty and we are more sexually active than at any time in history."

"Also," Diana says, "diminution of the corpus callosum—"

"Diana," Mother warns.

Diana smiles at Mother's exasperation, a warming, welcome sight in the somber atmosphere of this room. I believe it is the first actual smile I've seen. She touches the sides of her silver-white hair briefly as she explains, "Our two cerebral hemispheres hold a core of nerve fibers—white matter, gray matter. A front-to-back fissure divides the cerebrum's two hemispheres. One hemisphere is dominant—it holds speech and thought centers and determines our right- or left-handedness. The other one performs a complexity of other functions. The corpus callosum is the band of white matter that connects them."

"A kind of transmitter between the two?" I inquire. Among all my sisters, I am the least reluctant to ask questions; I have the least qualms about revealing my ignorance.

"Yes, it is, Minerva. It facilitates the integration of sensory data and responses from both sides of the body."

"Why would a thinner corpus callosum be significant?"

"We don't know that it is."

Scowling with impatience over this nonanswer, Mother asks, "Wouldn't it stand to reason that a thinner whatever-it-is would make integration more efficient?"

"Perhaps. Also perhaps less efficient because it may actually scramble transmission of the impulses. We're still trying to determine the answer by experiment," she adds, answering my next question, "but duplicating any human brain function is no simple matter. Our most sophisticated computers are finite and have all turned out to be inadequate replicators of the full capacity of the human brain."

Diana adds, "We continue to evaluate this evidence, but in all other respects there seems no evolutionary change. We've detected no mutation in our genetic code. Which is not to say there won't be over succeeding generations—it's far too early to tell."

"You refer to these children as members of the Unity," Hera says dourly. "A dubious inclusion when they want nothing to do with any of the philosophy or history we cherish."

Disturbed by what I've heard, I reflect that it is only to be expected the young will rebel. My sisters and I surely did, even against a personage like Mother. Albeit much of our rebellion consisted of mere mischief-making—led by the always audacious Hera—amid our normal individuation. "They were at the landing area to greet us," I point out, clutching at any strand of optimism. "They understood the meaning and importance of doing so. So you do communicate with them—"

"They understand what they decide to understand," Diana says with a touch of peevishness. "They pay no attention to our requests and do not answer our questions. We're the ones who lack understanding of them."

"Surely no one of you," I begin, "knew in advance they would acknowledge Mother with that strange vigil around her house—"

Mother snaps to attention, her glance raking around the table. "Did any of you have an inkling they'd do such a thing?"

"Not at all," Danya says with an audible sigh and with as much discomfort as one would expect from a senior security officer who had no way of preparing for so improbable an event. "Once they began to form into a group, we were, as usual, powerless to prevent them."

"Why," Tara says quietly, speaking for the first time in this meeting. "Why such intolerance of many customs and yet such adoration given to a personage they've not seen till yesterday?"

"I believe it was..." Trailing off, Danya looks even more uncomfortable. She goes on with seeming reluctance, "From the way they behaved, my theory is it was their acknowledgment of Mother as...the creator."

"The what?" Mother gasps. The rest of us gape at Danya.

I recover my wits. "Well, in a sense you are a creator, Mother, since we're all your progeny. Danya, you don't mean...a creator beyond that, you don't mean a, a..." I cannot bring myself to say the word.

"Godhead?" Olympia supplies, speaking up for the first time. "Danya—is Mother a god to them?"

An elaborate shrug of Danya's powerful shoulders conveys that she has offered all the theory she can about this latest action from our baffling newest generation.

"We don't know," Diana offers simply. "There is so much we don't know."

"Vesta." I turn to the woman who is our premier psychologist. Of all nine of Mother's daughters, she is the one who inherited Mother's diminutive height. But not those breasts. Only Venus comes close in that category. "Vesta, I realize you've been back a day—"

"Yes, only a day," she replies in the voice that has lost none of its sweet calm and clarity over the decades. "But it's my priority. It's by far the most pressing problem facing our world—"

"One of them," mutters Danya from next to me.

"And I'm already in consultation with colleagues. I can state categorically that their behavior is classically, indisputably tribal—"

"Their own tribe," Danya mutters again.

"And while conflict with us exists because of our expectations of them, it does not appear to exist among themselves. Which is not only atypical, but virtually unheard of in any sociological study. All tribes have some level of conflict."

Venus leans forward over the table to focus her azure gaze directly on Mother, then in turn on Megan, Olympia, Tara, and myself. "They're like a hive of bees in their cooperation and conformity among themselves, their lack of intrinsic conflict—"

I blurt the thought as it occurs to me: "Could they be telepathic?"

"Yes," Diana tells me. "We suspected that from the start. And explored the possibility for quite some time. We think they are to some extent. They have a form of instant communication but it appears rudimentary—they rarely act in concert like they have with Mother. At least not that we've ever seen. They seem to share little of our empathic capacity. Their behavior is highly individualistic, from earliest age, very unlike the rigid roles and circumscribed behavior of members of a beehive. There seems little connection among them when it comes to behavior—the proof being, there have been many deaths among them, and they have been unwilling to do anything to prevent their dying—"

"*Deaths*? They *let* each other die?" I gasp, and hear similar sounds of horror from Vesta, Olympia, and Tara. Megan's reaction is tears.

This is inconceivable. It has been three centuries since prenatal and postnatal gene therapy solved every physical and mental deficiency affecting newborns and children. Life now ends in adulthood, not childhood, by natural causes, by suicide, or through the occasional accident that can rob life from anyone of any age. "Why? Why would *any* of them *die*?"

"We don't know," Diana says, despair in her voice. "They seem healthy enough from the womb—in fact they radiate physical and emotional health. They remove themselves from our care typically when they're four, at most five years old—and they will not submit to physical scans and do not report any physical abnormality. Of the four generations born since our arrival, the deaths occur invariably among the second generation. We don't know why. We simply cannot account for their deaths."

"How many?" whispers Megan, hands clasped.

Demeter finally breaks the silence to answer. "We've found seven hundred and twenty-seven."

More gasps. This is horrendous. The grief of the mothers who have lost these children is beyond imagination.

Demeter continues. "We know there must be more since we can only count those we find. Each one goes off by herself and simply…dies." Amid the soft sobs emerging from around the table, Demeter goes on, "Much of what we've learned about them is from these bodies we've been able to study."

For some time there is silence. Then Danya says bitterly, "What they have most in common is their complete rejection of us—they would rather die than ask for help, to have us perform the simplest act to save their lives."

I say the obvious: "I don't understand it. Of course you've tried to talk to them—"

"Minerva, how stupid can you be?" Hera snaps.

I don't reply because tears stream down her face and her body sags with anguish. Demeter says, "We know where the largest number of them live, but not how they live. Yesterday, when they assembled for the landing, this was by far the most we've ever seen of them in years. Occasionally, groups of them turn up here from time to time—we don't know why—and then move off. They won't be found."

"What do you mean, they won't be found?" I demand. This is a logical impossibility. We have technology that can pinpoint from vast distances in space the existence of life on a planet, its type, and precisely where it is.

"I've led parties of searchers to observe them," Danya says. "Most of them are on Amazonia—"

I nod. From my studies of Maternas I am familiar with that forbidding terrain.

"When we lock onto them with instruments they find it a simple matter to melt into a landscape that is virtually inaccessible," Danya concludes.

"We've caught them, of course—for what good it does. They do not respond or cooperate in any way."

"We don't know how they want to live?" Olympia asks. "What they want from us?"

"We don't know how they live," says Diana. "They want nothing from us—beyond wanting us to leave them alone."

Olympia whispers, "How many are there?"

"As of a year ago, about forty thousand."

A lost generation of forty thousand. I am chilled to the marrow.

PERSONAL JOURNAL OF JOSS

"There's a place..." Emerald begins. "It's something not remotely in your plans for today."

I wait. Then venture, "Whatever you have in mind, I'd be glad to do it."

"Perhaps not all that glad," she murmurs, her gaze fixed on the terrain below. "I just...was thinking I'd like you to see it," she continues in a low tone. "It's...a place on Amazonia."

The intriguing equatorial continent we fly over now. Her doubtfulness further piques my interest. "I'm quite willing."

"It's not safe there, Joss. Even the landing is risky."

I gaze at the land below us. Amazonia, so named in honor of the women warriors of ancient times, is primordial territory, more than equal to another of its namesakes, the Amazon River delta on Earth before that irreplaceable jungle was laid waste in the twenty-first century. Amazonia remains uncharted, and from the air the reason seems clear: It looks virtually impenetrable; dense jungle interlaced with wild coral rivers and absent a main artery into the interior, like Earth's Amazon River. Its lush tropical forests shimmer intensely, exotically, with iridescent blue-green growth. I would love to set foot there, however briefly. "I've seen some studies of the continent. I'm aware of its risks," I tell Emerald.

"You know a great deal about our world," she says grimly. "But not as much as you may think."

She appears hesitant, to be having second thoughts about her proposal, and I confidently offer with considerable understatement, "I've been in risky situations before."

Again that slow smile that becomes an emerging radiance in the austerity of her face. "True. This would be child's play compared to the years of evading Theo Zedera and the role you took the day your Earth changed forever."

I laugh. "You too are well informed."

Her gaze lingering on me, she does not reply. Then she nods and turns her focus to plotting a flight path as the *Sarah Bernhardt* veers lower.

Emerald, much like Africa, gives care to the expenditure of words. Africa, synthesist par excellence by profession, absorbed masses of information, and when she spoke, it was a distillation from an enormous intellect. For Emerald, I sense her taciturnity as a rigidly disciplined inwardness that is not her fundamental nature.

We transect a vast jungle in our descent, slowing precipitously as we glide along a churning, coral river. Pressed back into my seat by the braking of our craft, I alternate between my view of the landscape flashing past, and Emerald, her face tense, eyes narrowed in concentration, lower lip clasped between her teeth as her fingertips dance over the multicolored sensors on the consoles before her.

The energetic pulsing of an alarm signals that a targeted landing area is close. As we swoop down to seemingly skim the rushing water of the river, I involuntarily suck in breath. We careen in over the river bank, hover for an instant, and then Emerald sets us down abruptly on a vast rock outcropping overhanging the river, a fine landing that cannot do more damage than perhaps a few scorch marks on the rock.

"You can unclench your fists now," she says with a grin.

Indeed, my knuckles are bone-white. "You're quite a pilot," I tell her.

"Scared me too," she says breezily, rising from her pilot's chair to lead me into the exit chamber.

We step out of the chamber into an avalanche of warm rain and a deafening cacophony of sound: the high *scree* of insects, the screams and calls of varied and vibrant wildlife. My hair is instantly plastered to my head, and I must wipe water from my eyes and employ both hands as a visor to make out the blue-green striations of thick jungle through the curtain of rain that pounds onto and ricochets off the ferrous rock on which we stand. Unless what Emerald wishes to show me is close by, finding our way through this blinding rain and then entering that towering maze of jungle looks every bit as daunting as landing here.

Emerald moves close to me to be heard over the uproar. "Set your E-Band on optimum," she orders as she programs her own wristband.

I obey, my adrenaline shooting to another level; her instruction amply indicates the danger of where we will venture.

She pauses at the edge of our rock, more to remember, it would appear, than to orient herself; visibility is no more than a few meters. As she leads the way, veering left, the sluicing rain has virtually rendered her slender form naked, so molded are her clothes to her body. She wears pants and a shirt again today, but they are ice blue in color, not last night's white, and to my dismay I realize she will blend into the jungle far more than I in my greenish Earth tones. I resolve to not separate myself from her by more than a meter.

As we come down the rock at the river line, an opening to the jungle appears, a trail, its trampled fern floor evidence of use by large creatures seeking water—on days unlike this one when they can simply lift their heads to the sky and drink. We enter a wide high tunnel of vines intricately entwined around blue-green trees with huge leaves, larger than the size of my body, and lush ferns with the girth of elephants. I feel suddenly hemmed in, claustrophobic, surrounded on all sides by danger. With each step I take I do not know what lies underfoot, and the height and denseness of the growth above us is graphically shown by the dimness of our passageway and the sudden cessation of rain. Only a few drops of the torrent falling a mere few meters behind us manage to penetrate the overhead canopy onto this trail.

Above us, on both sides of us, life screams and roars its defiant presence. Despite the current emitted from my wrist E-band, I stare anxiously around my feet for snakes. I am exceedingly grateful for this wrist-mounted device that will repel all wildlife within a ten-meter radius, discouraging it from approaching, much less attacking, and will even safeguard us from any species—such as primates—capable of hurling objects. From the width and height of this tunnel, the infuriated cries and trumpeting of retreat, some creatures around us must be sizeable indeed. The age of the dinosaurs, I comfort myself, had ended on this planet, a mere twenty million years ago, compared to the seventy on Earth. I do see one of the jungle denizens hastily retreating, and gasp as it slithers off through the vines: a dark blue snake fully a meter in circumference.

Emerald has spotted it too. "Twenty meters long at least," she tells me.

A reptile that size would either coil around and suffocate its prey, or swallow it whole, or both. I follow Emerald in increasing wonder and trepidation. What could she want to show me that would be meaningful enough to risk the landing and this excursion?

Emerald shakes water from her hair and clothes and I do as well; her shirt and pants quickly resume their customary elegant drape on her body, while the tendrils of her damp hair curl featherlike around her face.

My ears buzzing with the uproar of the raucous universe around us, I am aware that the air is warm. Beyond warm—so hot that my clothes are slow to adjust, and actually steam in the process, and will not, I realize, prevent the film of perspiration forming on my face from the heat and damp. I am assaulted by potent smells—the loamy, leafy, decaying, fecund, animal smell of verdant, living jungle, with heavy, almost cloying floral overtones. I see none of what I hear and smell; this forest primeval is of such density that I can peer several meters into it at most.

Emerald takes me by the sleeve to draw me near and brings her lips close to my ear to be heard: "We have less than two hundred meters to go."

I pick my way more easily along the trail beside her, knowing our destination is at hand.

The trail opens out to what can be termed a clearing only by comparison to the choked jungle from which we emerge. The stony, greenish soil here suggests its chemical composition contributed to the reduced growth density. Again the rain streams down on us, but it is quieter, and I can see farther into the steaming jungle, to hairy primate-type animals of varying sizes hanging from vines to peer down at us, to fur-backed small creatures that leap and hop around through the ferns at the periphery of our E-bands' range.

Emerald leads, but hesitantly now. Her head drops, and her chest heaves as if she is reluctant to proceed. More than reluctant—in distress. I take her arm gently. To my surprise she leans into me for support.

"It's the first time I've been back here," she says, her head turned to me as if she cannot bear to see what lies ahead.

"Do you want to go on?"

She answers by gripping my arm and striding into and through the clearing,

She halts in front of a group of vine-choked trees. Staring at a place on the forest floor, she says, "It was here. I found her here. And carried her back."

"Emerald," I say, "who?"

"Esme. My daughter. My beautiful daughter, Esme."

I do not need to have her tell me that our venturing here is a pilgrimage to a place of tragedy and loss. "Why was she here?" I ask.

"Many of them are here," she tells me.

"Who?"

"Our lost generations. She and Adira were among the first. The first to leave us. She died here. My daughter Esme, one of the first to die."

Shocked, I step back. *Deaths? Young women died here? How can that be?* I leave her to her meditations because I cannot imagine why this happened and because there is no consolation to be offered for the inconceivable loss of a child, only what support my presence may bring. Tears well at the thought of this slender woman bearing her dead daughter through that green tunnel we have just traversed.

She stands motionless. Then the weight of her own memories prove too much. I just barely manage to catch her as she collapses.

PERSONAL JOURNAL OF MINERVA

As we continue our informal meeting in the Council Chambers in Cybele, the mood continues to plummet as the situation is made ever clearer, ever bleaker to those of us who are newcomers and returnees to Maternas.

Mother no longer looks tired; she's exhausted, her tiny body slumping in her chair. But she sits up straight to aggressively ask, "Where are we now with them? What are we doing *now* to try and build a bridge to them?"

The initial response is glum silence. But there is an accompanying physical stirring of my sisters, and I read into it irritation if not anger, as if they are at pains to repress what might be quite sharp retorts. From everything they've conveyed thus far, they must resent Mother's insinuation that insufficient effort has been given to find a solution to this crisis.

Running a hand through her spiky blond hair, Danya addresses Mother. "A year ago we took a series of steps. One was asking Emerald to offer herself as emissary. In the absence of yourself and Megan, our reasoning was that since Emerald was closer in age to their generation and she was the firstborn of Megan, this might carry weight with them. She agreed to our request."

As she relates these details, Venus, Demeter, and Diana

seem to visibly shrink; stare down at the table, distress suffusing their faces. "We felt her involvement was appropriate for two additional reasons," Danya says. "Her twin daughters, Esme and Adira, were among those to show signs of...of the syndrome. Crystal's children did not. The generation that followed Esme and Adira's was completely engulfed, but it began with the second generation of births on Maternas. Of that second generation, not all were affected, but..." She spreads her hands. "With Emerald being Megan's firstborn and Emerald's own daughters among the affected, with the reverence accorded to Megan by everyone on this world..."

The distress in Danya's face and in her tone are palpable. She steals a glance at Megan, who does not look at her, does not look anywhere but at the table before her. I too gaze at Megan, in growing dread. "Such was our reasoning. We truly thought Emerald might have some...impact," Danya says softly. "Our instrument readings identified a large encampment of them on Amazonia. DNA tracings showed a probability of Esme and Adira being with them."

She touches the pad embedded in the center of our council table and brings up a slowly rotating hologram of the Amazonian continent. "I accompanied Emerald, of course. From our surveys and visual sightings, we knew they were on difficult if not inaccessible terrain." A new hologram: iridescent blue-green jungle dissected by rushing coral rivers. "To reach them we faced having to make a perilous pinpoint landing on a rock outcropping on the Vanessa River in Amazonia. Which we did. All of you in this room who know Emerald also know about her self-confidence. You won't be surprised she insisted on proceeding toward the area of our readings by herself. She was gone a day..."

Danya's shoulders heave with her sigh, and she closes her eyes, seemingly against memory, as she breathes out the next words: "She came back carrying Esme's body in her arms."

Megan sits motionless, unaware or uncaring of the tears

that course down her austere face to fall into her lap.

"Emerald has refused to speak of it since. Undoubtedly, she holds our interference to blame for Esme's death and perhaps other deaths as well." Again Danya sighs. "She may well be right."

I knew nothing of this fate of Emerald's daughter, or that she had two daughters. Nor, I am certain, was the news of this death imparted to Megan until well after the landing, after the ceremonies of greeting. I would certainly have known, had she been told any earlier. And I too would have taken the same decision to withhold the news until she had been reunited with her loved ones. Her unbroken silence throughout our meeting is no longer a mystery, nor that she has taken no part in this meeting beyond her physical presence. She is immersed in her grief for her daughter's pain and the two children—one dead, one missing—neither of whom she ever had a chance to see.

"Adira?" I ask. "The ones who were here yesterday, was Adira—"

"No," Danya replies. "We know nothing of her fate."

Mother gazes at Megan with anguish in her eyes. "Girls," she says firmly, "exactly what have we done since that time?"

Diana answers. "I thoroughly examined each body when I was given permission to do so." Pain inhabiting her sensitive features, she does not look at Megan. "A thorough examination down to the cellular level. I ran every possible test. Took samples of every tissue and body fluid, did gene-chip array, proteomics, PCR, mass spec, culture, biochemistry, histology, immunohistolchemistry—you name it, we did it before the interment at Nepenthe."

"So you've not examined living children, only their remains?"

"Yes, we have." Diana looks distressed, even embarrassed as she admits, "We captured some of them."

Mother is as astonished as I. But she only stares at Diana while I shake my head.

"Yes, Minerva," Diana says to me, anger in her tone. "Such was our desperation. We performed an act that is against our beliefs, against our charter, against everything we hold dear. Such was our desperation that we held a vote to override our charter of individual rights and our inviolate belief that the end never justifies the means. Such was our desperation that we agreed—unanimously—to take a group of them."

I bow my head to my sister. Had I been here, I would have cast one of those unanimous votes to do what they did.

"We used my preparations for captivity," Demeter says.

Of course they would. She is our premier meditech.

"It was planned and carried out under my supervision. A tranquilizer was injected while they slept. A sedative that would remove all awareness to well below the subconscious level. We moved in as a team and ran our tests and scans quickly and without moving them from where they lay. They would awaken never knowing anything had happened."

"And?" demands Mother.

Geneticist Diana takes over. "We found what we told you before—augmentation of the clitoral area and thinning of the corpus callosum, the band of white matter connecting their brain hemispheres. Also elevated levels of Estrova in two of them—so they've found a naturally occurring source somewhere for when they choose to conceive."

"Surely you have *some* idea of how they live. How they manage."

"Observation of them is no easy matter, Mother. They're so adept at concealing themselves that orbital observation is useless, and it requires instrumentation to locate them. Most are in Amazonia and wouldn't lack for food—"

"You say all of them were here for the landing. How did so many thousands of them get here from such a distance?"

"We're not sure," Diana says. "Among the many things we don't know about them is how they learned of your return. If they found out at the same time we did, though, they had a lot of time—the weeks it took for you to make your way through our solar system—to make the journey here, and they must have taken some flitters with them—"

Diana makes reference to the multitudes of small, sun-powered conveyances we use for easy transportation around our continent. Freely available for any of the Sisterhood to take anywhere, they are designed for two people, can be easily modified to hold more, and are used mostly within our own area of Femina, but they could be implemented for intercontinental journeys if one did not mind their relative slowness compared with other, more aptly designed craft, and the sheer tedium of making such a trip.

Megan finally speaks, her calm, bell-toned voice filling the chamber. "Diana, you said before that thinning in the corpus callosum might make integration of brain activity less efficient because it may actually scramble transmission of the impulses."

"Correct."

"Is it possible then, that this generation has taken an evolutionary step backward?"

"It's entirely possible. It's one of the reasons we took the next step. A year ago."

"A year ago?" I ask, a chill in my bones.

"Yes," Diana replies. "A year ago."

The face of Celeste, my daughter, rises into my mind. Celeste, who awaits my return from this gathering to tell her what her future may hold.

"A year ago, when all of us stopped having children," Diana continues.

Celeste's worst nightmare has just taken form in this room.

"There is no point having more, Minerva. Until we definitively know what coming here has done to our offspring."

PERSONAL JOURNAL OF OLYMPIA

"Nothing has changed," Diana utters in despair. "Nothing—in the entire year since we made our decision to give birth to no more children who will walk away from us into an existence we're no part of."

There has been little I could contribute to this profoundly disturbing discussion, beyond sympathy, and this, however heartfelt, would consist of unwelcome clichés not remotely adequate in the face of the immensity of the tragedy visited upon this world. I have allowed Minerva to speak for me, and I have instead concentrated on listening attentively, and holding my counsel until I have perhaps something of substance to offer. Tara has been equally silent.

"Something *has* changed, Diana," I venture. "We have arrived here. Which means," I hasten to add, "because of Mother their behavior pattern altered—"

"And reverted right back," Venus retorts. But there is mourning in her voice, and she looks at me with faint hope I'll have something additional and useful to offer.

"They gave us some information in the process," I contend. "Which—"

The room shakes...

An earthquake...

Shaking us violently...
Going on and on... It's enormous!

It is an hour or so later. I am still trying to reassemble my wits, much less my composure.

Erika has entered our council chambers at our urgent request. Standing next to where Mother sits gingerly at the head of our table, Erika's undisciplined riot of gray hair is a symbol of the emotional dishevelment we all feel. She addresses us grimly: "We were lucky. This time."

Calling up the holograph of our continent of Femina and the geological schematics of our colony of Cybele, our geoscientist uses a laser light to draw a circle around a deep layer. "The earthquake was centered here, seven miles under us. It registered eight point seven on all our scales—"

My own gasp is but one of many from around our council chambers table.

"Yes. You hardly need me to confirm this is the strongest earthquake in our history, exceeding the seven point six recorded four months ago. Had it occurred even a mile closer to the surface, our landscape, rugged though it is, would have transmogrified, and some of us—" She breaks off, then says, "Our lives would have been in jeopardy."

"What you meant to say is, some of us would have died," Hera states bluntly.

Erika nods. "Yes, esteemed Hera. Possibly quite a lot of us."

I feel fortunate to have lived through this one. The initial jolt of the quake pitched me violently from my chair into Demeter, who was herself falling on Hera. We no sooner staggered to our feet than the next jolt hurled us off them again. Megan and Danya, with the advantage of lesser age, maintained their balance but still staggered drunkenly about as the room bucked and shook. Our massive council table lurched over the chamber floor as if it had acquired misshapen wheels, divesting itself of fruit and delicacies and flagons of water, menacing life and limb with its every lunge.

All of us had the simultaneous thought: *Mother.* To protect her at whatever the cost. As we struggled toward where she lay with her arms covering her head, motionless on the floor, Megan reached her first, lifting her slight figure into her arms and then somehow managing to hoist herself and her precious burden onto the careening table. A brilliant stratagem since riding the bucking stallion of our table was preferable to being menaced at floor level by its every swerve.

Hearing shrieks of fright from outside our walls, all of us maintained the presence of mind to resist our immediate instinct to run from the council chambers. Worse peril might await in the form of landslide, falling rock and debris. Here, beyond our marauding table, no walls would collapse, nor would the ceiling come down; considerable strength and elasticity had factored into their construction.

When the shaking blessedly stopped an eternity later, again our first concern was Mother. But she was already extracting herself from Megan's protection, patting her on the cheek, and telling the rest of us, "I had the good sense not to fight city hall." Another of her quaint twentieth-century idioms. To our uncomprehending faces, she impatiently explained, "I exercised the good sense to keep still till the shaking stopped."

"The duration of the quake was a minute and five seconds," Erika informs us.

"Is that all?" Mother says, and she speaks for everyone.

It was a terror that lasted well beyond its own particular eternity, until wrist bracelets buzzed all over Femina and Maternas with contacts from loved ones. Not all of us in this room have made certain her loved ones are safe, including myself—I don't know about Ceeley—and including Tara, who has left to seek news of Joss; but there are no preliminary signs or reports of injury beyond bruising, no serious damage, and we have resumed our meeting, feeling even more impotent in the face of forces we cannot seem to fathom, much less control.

"What is our status, Erika?" Mother inquires. She appears calm and alert. Our heightened adrenaline level has expunged exhaustion from us all. "Will we have a recurrence?"

"Possibly. Not likely. The greater likelihood is a series of lesser aftershocks as the strata settle. But this area has turned out to be so anomalous, its seismological patterns so out of conformance with other areas on Maternas and to all our known science, I can't make any confident prediction."

"So this could happen again," Mother says dourly.

"Yes."

"And it could be even worse next time."

"If there is a next time and if it's closer to the surface..." Erika does not finish.

"Is it possible *they* could have done it?"

It is Minerva who voices this question, and sadly, no one appears surprised, objects to the question, or needs to inquire who "they" are. Our children—*our children*—have become "they."

"It is not possible," Erika states immediately, flatly.

"Erika, put my skepticism down to the fact that in just the last hour enough years have been subtracted from my life expectancy to catch me up with my sisters. It seems most coincidental that one day after we arrive—"

"It is indeed coincidence," Erica states evenly. "Esteemed Minerva, the massive forces needed to unleash—"

"Erica," Minerva interrupts sharply, "what I understand is this. We don't know what they're capable of. Perhaps we were misled as to why they all gathered here yesterday and then went away. Perhaps they do have powers. Perhaps all of them working in concert—"

"Not possible," Erika avers and then adds in a more conciliatory tone, "We'd have seen other evidence of telekinesis prior to this one while they tested their powers. The return to Maternas—it's the first time we've ever seen them act in concert."

"Perhaps not. You yourself say the seismic activity is an anomaly—"

"Minerva raises a good point," I interject. "We ourselves used similar methods as a means of self-defense while we were hidden on Earth."

"Yes, Olympia. But you were acting in self-defense. We represent no threat to our children. Why would they do this? I can't imagine why they would think we're any threat to them. Why would they want to harm us? We may not understand what's happening on our planet, but it seems clear these are natural occurrences. If the newest generation had powers of telekinesis, we would have seen them. They would have tested them long before this in far lesser ways."

"I still say they may have. Maybe we just didn't..." Minerva shrugs, subsides into unhappy silence.

"Are there other questions?" Erika surveys our faces. "I'll be making additional assessments and will transmit my data," she says formally and takes her leave.

"Olympia," Mother says gently, bringing the meeting back to order, and everyone's attention back to me. "My dear, you were making a point before we were so rudely interrupted."

"Perhaps an important one. I was suggesting this generation reached out, to you, Mother—"

"But only to her, Olympia," Venus says, resuming her argument.

"Not true." And I shake my head in emphasis. "I was on the platform at the landing site. I observed them."

Who would not? They were stunningly beautiful young women. They drew everyone's gaze. Little had I realized at the time that their physical attributes were not the only reason the women of this world were so fixated on them. I continued, "I noticed they hardly touched anyone—"

"They rarely do," Demeter confirms. "If anyone touches

them, they mostly convey revulsion—they become rigid as statues."

"They touched Joss. Reached out to her. Three of them touched her, took her hands in greeting."

"Surely they did that to others, Olympia," Minerva argues. "After all, they were there by the thousands."

"Possibly they did. But there were only a few of us arrivals, and we were all in one place. I tell you I watched them—who wouldn't? I thought it very odd that newcomers were the only ones they touched.."

Mother looks bewildered. "Why? Why would they do this?"

"I've been thinking about it," I say. "Of our returning party, Joss is among those closest to their generation in age."

"What are you suggesting?" Mother fixes me with a gaze of sharp interest.

"With what's at stake, we have nothing to lose," I tell her. "Perhaps we should try sending other emissaries, especially someone like Joss who has no child involved, as Emerald did. Maybe their touching her is an indication she may have some effect. She has the most tenuous of ties to this world. She has no children among this newest generation. She has the advantage of emotional distance. I have the same advantage. We should both go and try to establish communication."

Megan is staring at the pad in front of her and holds up a hand for silence. Her expression is distraught, but her voice is calm. "We'll have to find her first, Olympia. Tara has just reported that Joss and Emerald are missing."

My immediate thought is the earthquake, that they've been buried...

"They took one of our craft early this morning for exploration. They haven't been seen since."

PERSONAL JOURNAL OF JOSS

"Thank you, Joss," Emerald says softly, sitting back against a thick tree trunk entwined in thick ivory-blue vines.

On my knees before her, I sit back on my heels and simply nod.

"When I was here before—that's when I had every reason..." Emerald looks away, into the jungle that surrounds us with its alien wildness, its engulfing cacophony. "I don't know how I...her weight, the weight of my grief—I couldn't carry either one, much less both. Bringing her out of here, carrying her all the way back to where we landed today—it was impossible. Yet somehow I did it."

I make no reply. No words are adequate, and I sense it is not words she requires, only my presence. She does not look at me but sits with hands clasped around her knees, looking into a place of darkest memory. I remain kneeling before her; it feels appropriate to be this close to her, in the same posture as after I caught her body in my arms as she fainted, after I lowered her to the ground, an arm circling her shoulders. Rain continues to solemnize this place of loss and tragedy.

Leaning her head back into the vines behind her, she reaches to her slender throat and pulls up a chain of fine ivory links from within her wet shirt, lifts the chain over her head, and lowers it into coiled segments in her palm. She brings both hands together as if to warm the chain, as if her own body had been insufficient to the task.

She forms her hands into a cup holding the chain. "Megan placed this around my neck when I was born. I wore it till Esme and Adira were born, then I placed it around Esme's neck because she was first to emerge. I thought she'd do the same the day she had her own first child…" She says this in an expulsion of words, a compulsion to explain. "But she…she took it off. She left it when she…"

After one final, lingering gaze at the chain, she picks it up and holds it between a thumb and an index finger, letting it fall to its full length. Then she lowers it into the damp mossy undergrowth beside her. She folds it in, brushing over it additional wet loam and leaves, smoothing, then laying a gentle hand over the place as if to impart her own living energy. She closes her eyes and sits motionless; I kneel just as quietly before her.

She finally pulls her hand away, turns it over and gazes down at the bluish stains on her palm. "When I was here before, all I could think about was carrying her out, taking her back with me. I left nothing to mark…I needed to come back, to leave something…something of her in the place where she…she…I needed to return. But I couldn't. Till now." She attempts a smile, and even wanly succeeds. "I couldn't come alone. It seems I needed someone who knows nothing of what's happened, who's not been a part of the sorrow of our world, to accompany me. I am deeply in your debt, Joss."

I know nothing about the sorrow of this world that she refers to, but this is not the time to ask. I say to her, "You owe no debt to me. I am honored to accompany you. I am honored that you brought me here."

She looks at me, and there is a new emotion I cannot read in her luminous green eyes. "My mother, Laurel, came here as a survivor of a damaged spaceship," she tells me, a fact I already know. "She showed me her personal journal about the events of those days. I've never forgotten what happened when Megan took her to Nepenthe, where my daughter is now, the place where we inter all the dead of our Sisterhood. Like you, Laurel was an off-worlder; like you, she said those exact words to Megan in a place of death: 'I am honored that you brought me here.'"

Then, like a pent-up dam finally breaking, she sobs. And I move quickly to her, to take her in my arms.

I draw her close to soothe her trembling, for whatever comfort my body can provide in the falling rain. Her head comes to just above my chin, her dark hair a wet silken sleekness against my face, and my lips touch her forehead as she turns her face into me.

Her voice is muffled by sobs: "It's my fault she died."

"No," I whisper. It can't be true.

"If I hadn't come here to find her, she wouldn't have died. She wouldn't have believed she had to die. To make herself into a terrible message I had to carry back...She didn't want me to take her, Joss. She wanted to say something to me, but when I saw she was dying I had to take her, I had to...She expended all her strength trying to stop me. She died in my arms while I was carrying her..."

I hold her close, wanting to absorb her escalating sobs into my own body, as if I can somehow fully shelter her in my arms, shelter her from the rain and from everything that torments her.

For the first time since Africa left my universe, my heart has opened again. So much so that I have to ask myself, even in these circumstances: *Is my role in life to always be the comfort of women carrying immense burdens of grief and guilt? Women lost in their own universe of sorrow and forever unattainable?*

Asking these questions brings me an answer, but it is to another, unasked, question. The answer is: As much as I feel for Tara, I do not and cannot love her in the way I so consumingly loved Africa, or in the way I have begun to love this woman I hold in my arms. Even if, again, it turns out that that love is hopeless.

It is as I experience this epiphany that I look up.

Behind Emerald, eyes stare at us. Many of them. Coral eyes with ivory pupils.

PERSONAL JOURNAL OF MINERVA

Two more aftershocks have rocked our chamber. In comparison to the psychic upheavals already visited upon me, these geological manifestations seem far lesser. I feel shaken and pummeled and bruised by everything I have heard and felt and witnessed—indeed, from the moment I landed on this planet.

A society of women on its own world has always been the most sublime daydream, an ultimate, seemingly impossible Utopia. The actuality, after the fifty-five years of existence of such a world, is more like a nightmare. The kind of world we sought and found, the seeds of philosophical idealism we planted—what we reap now is a harvest of tragedy.

My fervent wish is to flee back to Earth, with all its flaws, with my beloved Christa, our precious Celeste, and all my sisters. This seditious thought I put away from me because all my wisdom and whatever else I can offer are needed here. But the thought has only been put away—and just for now. It has not been dismissed.

Trying to settle my nerves now that the latest tremors have subsided, I drain what water has not been flung from my goblet by the rocking of our chamber and bring my attention back to our meeting.

"They have not responded to our calls," Megan says, as if

she has not noticed the latest aftershock. And perhaps she has not. "The craft they took was the *Sarah Bernhardt.*"

"Where are they?" asks Hera.

"We don't know," Megan replies, staring at the screen before her, her fingers moving over keys.

"Impossible," retorts Hera. "The beacon—"

"Is not operative," Megan states.

"Impossible. It's—"

"Indestructible. Yes, I know, esteemed Hera. But we're picking up no signal."

"How can that be!" Hera demands, rising out of her chair and marching over to where Megan sits at her screen. "It's constructed of elements impervious to—"

"We don't know how that could happen," Danya says distractedly, busy at her own screen, "but it has. Right now we're checking atmospheric traces of their flight path... Amazonia," she announces triumphantly. "All aerial traces end at...Amazonia." Her fingers fly over her keys. "On the..." She looks up at Megan, her face suddenly stricken. "On the Vanessa River, where we were before when Esme—"

"Yes," Megan says. "She's gone back there..."

"To where her daughter died," Vesta says gently. "It's understandable."

"And taken Joss with her," Olympia says, distress in her face and her voice.

Megan says, "That we've lost communication is...we need to scramble a team."

"We can't," Danya says sharply. "We can't," she repeats more softly and raises a hand before Megan can begin her protest. "We need an aerial surveillance report first. Megan, these are the reasons..."

Again she brings up a hologram of the Amazonian continent, picks up a laser pointer. "Where their trail ends is here, at the Vanessa River. There's only one landing site—right here." She circles a point down the river.

"*One?*"

"One. The river currents are so swift and the jungle so dense that a hundred-meter rock outcropping on the river is the only place a craft can set down. If the *Sarah Bernhardt* is already on it we can't—"

"Another kind of small craft then."

"There is no other kind, Megan. In your absence we've not produced anything more advanced than our flitters—we've not had to. Flitters are far too fragile to drop from orbit, and if we take one from here, at their speed it'll take two days for the journey. Give us just an hour," Danya pleads. "We'll have precise imagery from our drones."

Frustrated, Megan gets up from her chair and begins to pace, her hands clenched into fists.

"We've already released them, Megan. Please, just one hour—"

"Diana," Mother says calmly, "you told us the greatest number of our youngest women are on Amazonia."

"Yes, Mother. They are."

"And, Olympia, you suggested that Joss may be a useful emissary."

"Not in quite this manner," Olympia replies with a grimace.

"Nonetheless it's happened."

Mother rises to her feet, a signal this meeting is over. "I've always had confidence in all my girls. We've been in serious situations before—"

Not like this one, I say to myself.

"I'm sure you girls can manage," she pronounces her mantra serenely, and, gathering her green robe around her, takes her leave of our council chambers.

"Danya," Megan says, "let's take the *Marie Curie,* just in case. We'll already be on our way while the reports come in."

"Done," Danya says, leaping to her feet.

"I'm going with you," Olympia declares as she too gets

up, adding before either Megan or Danya can protest, "Joss is my protégé. She is as dear to me as Emerald is to you, Megan."

Now that the dimensions of what lies before us have been made clear, I also stand and inform Megan and Danya, "I am Minerva the historian. I too will accompany you."

PERSONAL JOURNAL OF JOSS

We are surrounded. By twelve magnificent-looking young women, none of whom by my reckoning are a day older than myself. They are as scantily clad as when I first saw them after my arrival on this world, with a band securing their breasts and rough sandals on their feet. Having materialized from the Amazonian jungle, they circle us and gaze at us with their mesmerizing coral eyes. Emerald and I can only stare helplessly back.

I finally tear my attention away, to grip Emerald's arm, increasing my pressure until she turns to me. The bewilderment on her face tells me she knows nothing more than I do about why these women are here, what they might want from us.

Having taken up position around us, the twelve stand motionless, oblivious to the rain that streams from their hair down their faces, over their breasts, down their arms and legs. If they intend us harm, they have brought no means with which to inflict it. Even so, their youth and superior numbers obviate the need for any weapon.

I venture, "Who are you?"

They give no indication they have heard me.

"Who are you?" I demand in my loudest tone.

Not so much as an eyelid flickers in response.

I turn slowly, gazing at each of them. They display no sign of friendliness—or any other emotion. No hint of recognition of Emerald. No sign of hostility, either in their faces and surely not in the easy grace of their posture. There is nothing whatever in their faces I can read. Or in their glorious bodies that range in hue from golden bronze through mahogany. They stand motionless, alarmingly beautiful statues, gleaming in the rain.

I focus on the woman directly in front of me. She meets my gaze unwaveringly, but there is no other movement in her face other than the intermittent blinking of her eyelids over her coral eyes.

I suddenly wave a hand in her face. She reacts: not with resentment, amusement, or any kind of emotion that virtually anyone would display had someone made so impudent a gesture, but merely with several rapid eye blinks.

Emerald speaks: "Who are you?"

No response.

"Do you know my daughter?"

No response.

"My daughter, Esme?"

No response.

"My daughter, Adira?"

I manage to spot a flicker of recognition at this name in the eyes of the woman across from me; then impassiveness again.

"Why are you here?" I demand. "What do you want from us?"

No response.

Since they show no sign of wishing to communicate, nor of moving away, it seems pointless if not ridiculous to remain as we are. The circle they've formed is a loose one, and so I take Emerald's arm and walk us toward the jungle—simply to see what will happen. Only to have four women join arms to bar us. One question answered. Even though I don't understand the answer.

I turn us around, begin walking us in the direction of our ship, and this time we are allowed to move unrestricted between two women forming their circle.

"They want us to leave," I tell Emerald.

"I don't want to, Joss," she says, pulling her arm from my grasp. "Not if Adira is nearby."

I can hardly argue. In her place I too would seize any opportunity, however slender, to locate a daughter who's missing, even perhaps to glean whatever insight possible into the one lost to a death inexplicable and agonizing.

"They mean us no harm," she says

I nod. "I'm not eager to leave," I tell her. "But our best course for now is a return to the *Bernhardt*." I tap a finger once on my wrist communicator.

Emerald's eyes meet mine in wordless understanding. Our wrist communicators lack sufficient range to transmit from this continent, and she too sees the wisdom of contacting our Unity, and her mother Megan, before this, whatever it is, proceeds any further—however it is we are meant to proceed.

We have few options. Even if the women hadn't stopped us we could hardly have ventured farther into a jungle unknown to us—and to what purpose? Returning to the ship will open our communications and give us the choice to leave if that seems advisable or necessary.

As we make our way across the clearing, we glance back. The women have formed into a loose phalanx, and follow us at a leisurely gait and distance.

We reenter the tunnel leading back to the river, and the *Sarah Bernhardt*. The women continue to follow, and I steal surreptitious glances back at them, as does Emerald. They show no overt signs of watching us, nor do they appear to be communicating with each other, although it's difficult to be certain amid the din of the jungle. If they seem not to be conversing among themselves, they walk in close groupings of two or three, and there is physical contact, clasped hands, casual caresses that seem playful, almost kittenish. They seem unconcerned about us.

We emerge at the river—and back into the downpour that has not lessened since we exited our craft. As we make our way to the rock outcropping, our followers continue their meander behind us, toward the *Bernhardt*.

Through the sheets of rain I make out the vague shapes of other young women clustered around our ship, some sitting on the rock.

"Joss! They're in the *Bernhardt*!" Emerald calls, raising her voice over the hissing downpour. She hastens toward them.

Pawing at the rain in my eyes, employing my hand like a visor as I stumble after her, I glimpse several women leaping down from the exit chamber of our craft, and I feel the same urgency as Emerald.

The women around our craft ignore us and make no sign of greeting to the women who have followed us from the clearing. I notice in passing that a few children are here, none younger than perhaps six. We rush into the exit chamber, shaking the wetness from our clothing.

None of the young women are inside, but it is immediately apparent that some have been: Equipment is obviously missing, beginning with the exit chamber's recessed door panel. Emerald immediately leaps to the cockpit to check for what is most vital, our solar instrumentation panel.

"Gone, Joss. It's all gone."

Our communication unit, our beacon—and an odd assortment of other non-flight-related equipment as well, lighting panels, even our flight chairs.

The *Sarah Bernhardt* is a grounded bird. With the rushing river alongside us, the impenetrable jungle behind us, our craft disabled, we have no way of leaving here, of communicating with anyone, of being rescued.

Emerald races from the *Bernhardt.* I follow.

"Where is it?" she screams above the thunder of the rain, flailing her arms. "What have you done with it?" Hers is the pure outrage of a pilot whose craft has been sabotaged.

Unsurprisingly, there is no answer. The women, if they have heard us, do not react and continue to totally ignore us. We are left with nothing but frustration. Perhaps they have destroyed everything, even the supposedly impervious, permanent signaling beacon present in all our aircraft that will direct an emergency party in case of mishap.

Seizing the arm of the nearest woman, a tawny-skinned blond, Emerald screams, "Speak to me!"

But the woman freezes under her touch.

Gently, I draw Emerald away, an arm around her shoulders, and try to calm her; she is shaking with rage. "*What* are they doing to us, Joss? Why have they done this? I don't understand anything they do!"

"I understand why they wanted us to come back here," I tell her.

"I'm glad somebody knows *something,*" she retorts. "Tell me, Joss."

"They wouldn't let us go into the jungle because they wanted us to come back here."

"Why? What for? We can't leave!"

"They wanted us to find that out. We wouldn't have known it unless we came back here. They want us to know they won't let us leave."

"Why?"

I shake my head.

My imparting some small degree of rationale to our circumstances seems to have calmed her. "Whatever the reason," Emerald says, "we're stranded."

We watch them—it's all we can do—and as the rain continues its constant thrumming, and even though I realize we are in a perilous and unknowable situation, I cannot help but admire them. Our clothes have been designed to protect our fragile bodies, to deflect and adjust to any weather. Their virtual lack of clothing is the better, more perfect adaptation. Indifferent to the esthetics of this particular landscape and its discomforts, or perhaps having very different esthetics and comfort standards from the generations before them on this planet, they have brought themselves from Femina to a climate that suits them, rather than needing to adapt to a climate that does not. Still, I wonder what they do if the nights here grow chill, as they do elsewhere on Maternas.

They make no attempt to conceal anything about their physical selves and are as unselfconsciously naked as any animal. Even though they clearly have no notions about decorum or mores, I have avoided looking at their genital area out of a sense of propriety I cannot shake.

They have surrounded us again. Not a circle this time. One group has formed ahead of us, one behind. Perhaps twenty in each group. The one ahead of us turns its collective back to us and moves away toward the jungle. The group behind us crowds us, as if they wish to follow the leading group and we are impeding their path.

We are being herded.

"They're taking us somewhere, Joss," Emerald confirms. I hear subdued excitement in her voice.

PERSONAL JOURNAL OF OLYMPIA

The Marie Curie comes out of low orbit, our trajectory having taken us over Amazonia. In our control room, Megan and Minerva flank Danya, our pilot; I sit on the other side of Minerva.

Amazonia has raised my Earth-based definition of what constitutes an equatorial continent to an entirely new level. From this altitude its surface appears to be a wiry tangle of unchecked ivory-blue growth intersected by coral ribbons, the tangle looking penetrable perhaps by insects and small animal species but not by humans. I now understand what Danya meant when she so darkly alluded to the difficulty of navigating any part of this continent because of its topography. The vegetation is so dense that magnifications of the land masses on my view screen show scant variation from my normal view from window panels of the control room. Our visual scanners lack the capacity for producing the ultrafine definition that our drones possess, and those definitions are coming through only now, meaningless frames of dense jungle blipping across my screen, and not quickly enough for either Megan or myself.

I demand impatiently, "Why this interminable sequencing? Why does this have to take so long? Why don't we have permanent drones in orbit?"

"Esteemed Olympia, we have no need," Danya says softly.

I nod in embarrassment, having been caught out in forgetting that this world has nothing in common with Earth and its militaristic history, its unrelenting mistrust among nations, its constant hostile surveillance of neighboring territories. Silenced, I follow the images, programmed as they are for focus on our one area of interest, arriving in segments from the drones.

Finally, finally I see a wide, raging river. "The Vanessa," Danya confirms and begins freezing each image we receive for closer inspection.

Then at long last, the rock outcropping. And on it the *Sarah Bernhardt*. No sign of wreckage on the rain-soaked surface of the rock, only the few scorch marks to be expected from a landing. We all exhale in unison: The craft appears intact. I feel faint with relief.

"It would appear they are safe," Danya offers cautiously.

I choose not to speak my thought: *Not necessarily.* Our evidence doesn't extend nearly that far.

"How long have they been gone?" Megan asks briskly as she magnifies and scrutinizes readings of one area after another on the exterior of the *Sarah Bernhardt*.

"They departed Femina at midmorning," Danya answers. "Analysis of trace properties of their trail show they landed here in late afternoon. It's now dusk. Emerald and Joss have been on the ground approximately…four hours."

"We can do nothing after nightfall," Megan muses. "We must act now."

I am mystified as to how she thinks we can "act now," regardless of the time of day or night; we cannot land here unless we burn off a considerable swath to create a landing area—an action that would be in violation of the central provisions of our charter.

But Megan's daughter is down there. She may contemplate such a violation, but if she proposes it I will overrule her, as will the two other people on our craft. The life of none of us justifies damage to the planet—a lesson learned very late on the planet I have left. Surely she isn't thinking of…I voice my fear: "Are you considering destroying the *Bernhardt* so we can land?"

She throws me an amazed glance. "That's a totally unacceptable action. Our readings show life-forms in the area. Emerald and Joss may be in the craft."

Yes. Perhaps hurt, I think, anxiety rising in me again. An image of Joss rises in me: her strong, sturdy yet supple body with its superb athleticism, her clear dark-blue eyes—and most of all, that untimely maturity in the handsomeness of her face. After all Joss has been through already in her young life, I never dreamed that coming here would plunge her once more into extreme jeopardy.

"The beacon," Minerva says worriedly. "Why is there no beacon?"

"That's what most puzzles me," Megan says calmly. "We need to land."

Yes. But we cannot. We cannot leave the *Marie Curie* in orbit and take our light solar-powered flitters to the surface—they're not designed to be operative from this altitude.

With an economy of motion. Megan brings up a hologram of Maternas over her console and sketches coordinates on it with her laser pen. Then, indicating a speck beside a continental land mass, she says, "Danya, you can set down there—on Gearhart Island off the coast of O'Connor. We can get a few hours of sleep en route. Then take our flitters. By my calculations we can leave Gearhart Island at two and be back here by dawn's first light. We can land right beside the *Sarah Bernhardt.*"

I gaze at her admiringly, as do Danya and Minerva. I see again why she was given the mantle of leadership during the perilous times when our Unity departed Earth for this new world.

PERSONAL JOURNAL OF JOSS

Herded into the passageway leading away from the Vanessa River and the crippled *Sarah Bernhardt,* I feel as if I've stepped into the pages of a classic shipwreck tale. Except one of Earth's desert islands would be infinitely preferable to a steaming jungle of unknown denizens and unknown perils on an alien world. Could any shipwreck victim be any more displaced? Any more marooned?

No shackles restrict my hands or feet. I still have my recorder. I have not been searched, or even regarded as a captive, for that matter. Yet I transparently am one and walk beside another captive, a woman who has become vitally important to me, even though I have known her less than two days.

Now that we have entered the passageway, we are being shunted along in deliberate fashion by young women, some of them children, whose motives are incomprehensible. Nude but for breast bands, their hair no more cared for than the mane of a lion, their coral eyes gleaming preternaturally in the murkiness of the deeply overhanging jungle, they might be a tribe of Earth prehistory as they press us forward toward what purpose I cannot imagine.

I will not countenance the prospect of our capture having anything to do with one particular barbarism of pre–twenty-first century Earth. Only four generations removed from the women who are their progenitors, they could not have devolved so swiftly into the ultimate primitiveness of cannibalism. *Still, they are as remote, as unreachable as if they were creatures*—I smile wryly as I complete my thought—*from another planet.*

"Tell me about them," I say to Emerald.

Her response is a dubious look at them, then at me.

"They give no sign they can hear us," I argue, "much less understand what we say. Whatever we're facing, Emerald—I need you to give me some context."

She moves closer, to pitch her voice more directly to me over the jungle clamor. "My two daughters, Esme and Adira, were among the first to be affected. When they were born their combined motile and sessile ova predicted a polygenic inheritance pattern of four dominate alleles—"

"So their eyes would be light brown." This is basic biology—I don't need quite so much context.

"Instead they were coral. Tinged—barely—with light brown. And the pupils were ivory. We didn't notice any changes in their exterior genital area—those came later, during puberty. Laurel and I took them immediately to Diana, our chief geneticist."

"Yes." I met this member of the Inner Circle the previous night—which seems days ago—at the fete for our arrival.

"Their DNA tests and genetic patterns showed no mutation." She shakes her head. "We put it down to the obvious factors."

With an ivory-blue jungle around me, an unnavigable coral-colored river behind me where our craft sits, I can understand why Diana would assume the cause to be external, the result of consuming the food and water on this alien world. I say, "Meaning the changes were environmentally based."

"Correct. Diana assured me it was not genetic and I should not be concerned. I assume you know we have communal rearing of our children."

"Of course. We did the same during our two years in Sappho Valley."

"I gave birth when I was sixteen. It's when most of my generation on this world chose to have our children—"

Why so early? I wonder, but know better than to interrupt her.

"The two girls seemed fine, no different from anyone their age—many of them had the coral and ivory eye color. Crystal's daughters didn't but other children born in their generation did. All of them were bright...happy, playful. We have a very wide-ranging educational process, and all them were tremendously interested and involved—even more so than my generation. We congratulated ourselves," she says bitterly. She trudges along with her head down, as if lost in her memories. "They were all so unusually beautiful. We thought everything about them came from the gift we'd given them of being born free into a world of bounty, without any of the societal pressures of Earth. Then they—everything—just...stopped."

She seems so absorbed in her melancholy memories that for a time I leave her there, especially since I am watching the oldest women around me vanish into the jungle. They quickly reappear, having collected huge leaves from the jungle trees, and are folding them into an efficient, compact mass they can carry under one arm. For what purpose? Certainly not for use as clothing. To eat? To smoke? I doubt the latter since they appear to be paragons of health.

Finally, what I need to know at this moment again intervenes, and I ask Emerald, "What do you mean, stopped? Is that when things changed?"

"*Changed* doesn't begin to describe it," she says grimly. "We tried our best to account for it as some kind of generational rebellion. I was very rebellious too. So was my sister, Crystal. So was everybody my age."

"Megan and all the visitors to Earth were very anxious about your generation."

She smiles wryly. "Compared to Esme and Adira, we were models of comportment. Then they had their own daughters, Tauna and Kizza. Their eyes were much more predominantly coral. At puberty it turned out that their clitoral development was even more pronounced. Again Diana told us these were physical manifestations without a genetic trace—these were not gene-based mutations. They began to talk very early—at four months—and advanced very rapidly. But then at age two both little girls stopped talking. By age three they'd stopped listening. We determined their hearing was perfectly intact. But they wouldn't obey, and we tried everything short of corporal coercion. At age four they rejected anyone's touch, even their birth mother's—to the extent of refusing to breathe if anyone persisted. And at age five they began to leave us, to simply disappear. It did us no good to intervene and bring them back. Unless we put them in restraints, they would leave again."

"And their mothers?"

"Colluded," she says heavily. "When these newest children were born, that's when our world turned upside down, Joss. Esme and Adira became more and more withdrawn—as if they were being pulled into the strange half-life of their children. When their children began to leave, they helped them, they went with them."

"You couldn't get them to explain any of this?"

"It was as if they didn't know how. As if they couldn't understand what we wanted from them."

"After your daughters left, when you saw Esme again, how long had it been?"

"Ten years."

Sobered by this synopsis, I walk silently, especially now that we approach the place of the freshest agony, where Emerald placed the chain to commemorate her tragic reunion with Esme.

Crossing the clearing, I look back at the women behind

me. This time I notice the color differences in their eyes. The younger the woman, the more intense and vivid the coral hue.

As we approach the density of jungle that will soon envelop us, I realize that since we've been under the control of these women, we have tacitly entrusted our personal safety to them and lost all disquiet about jungle predators—in unconscious recognition that in this chosen environment of our captors, if they feel safe, then so should we.

But I have not adjusted the setting on my E-band. Impossible. Surely I must have changed the setting without realizing it. A surreptitious glance at my wrist shocks me. A glance at Emerald's wristband shows the same reading, a setting still at optimum range. How can this be? The force field from our E-bands would repel any creature smaller than an elephant approaching to within ten meters of us. Since these women don't wear their own neutralizing E-bands, they should have been hurled back when they first tried to approach us.

I take Emerald's arm, point to her wrist. She blinks in amazement, looks closer. Picks up my wrist to inspect my band. "They've been deactivated," she says. "But they can't be, they're light-powered." She shakes her wrist and then rechecks the band as if disbelieving the evidence of her own eyes. I've been told the bands are failure proof: they pick up any pigmentation other than black and will use it to operate even in total darkness.

"I wonder when they were deactivated," I say to her.

Her silence suggests she has the same thought I do, that when we first set our E-bands we assumed they were operational—we had no reason for verification. When we first departed the *Sarah Bernhardt,* did we walk all the way to the clearing without protection? And if so, why were we not menaced or even approached by any number and manner of wildlife?

More mystery to add to a rapidly growing tally. On that list is the question of why my recorder works when my E-band doesn't. I finger the fine chain around my neck, but verification is unnecessary; I feel the familiar faint pulse against my throat as the tiny recorder pendant absorbs the brain impulses of all that I see and think.

We are making our way into the jungle, the women all around us dispersing into the narrowest of pathways concealed in the heavy undergrowth. Our deactivated wristbands, our vulnerability, are more than ample incentive to stay close to them—the bigger and stronger the woman the better.

I reach for Emerald's hand and move ahead of her to lead the way, providing what little protection I can. Her slim fingers tighten convulsively around mine, and I can easily assume claustrophobia has been triggered in her as it has in me—who wouldn't feel it here? We could be in the smallest of caves, our light is so dim, and her slender body is virtually invisible behind me. We are being smothered by an ivory-blue riot of plant life that roughly accosts our bodies, that rattles and hums with insects and any manner of small animal life. Their calls reverberate all around us. The heat is intense and so are the fecund smells that fill up our nostrils. The undergrowth we traverse is well suited to heat, wet, and muted light—we have already witnessed a sample of the great volume of rainfall here, and I can only marvel at the possibilities of an ecosystem fed by soil containing a vastly extravagant level of fertilizing elements.

Fifty meters into this thicket, Emerald's hand convulsively clutching mine, I know four things. First, that while our clothing protects us from possible toxins or allergens exuded by the fronds and vines that constantly abrade us, the women ahead of us seem to require no protection. They remain unaffected, their skin dusted and lustrous with silvery pollens. The three other pieces of knowledge are more obvious: that Emerald and I are now completely lost, with no possible way of retracing our steps back to the clearing and to the *Sarah Bernhardt* other than managing to do so by accident; that any search mounted by our Unity will have next to no chance of success; and that I must focus all my concentration on protecting Emerald as we make our way to who knows where…

A kilometer or so into the jungle, our pathway becomes easier, the vines gradually thinning into ferns, bringing into visibility a larger number of women around us. If the canopy of trees above seems no less dense, it is higher above our heads and has allowed enough of a patter of rain to fall through and cleanse away the pollen. Our sensation of claustrophobia is lessened. Emerald and I can once again walk side by side. But I do not relinquish her hand.

She continues talking about her daughters and the nightmare leading up to her loss of Esme. Too preoccupied in assessing our risk to pay her the closest heed, I still hear the compulsive tone in her voice and know this has been a kind of catharsis as well as a distraction from the terrors of our suffocating terrain. But I have been unable to absorb more than the outlines of the detail she has been giving about her daughters' extreme alienation, their lengthening sleep pattern, other behavior patterns. Now something she has said snags my undivided attention. "*What* did you say was part of their diet?"

"Soil."

"They eat *soil*?"

She manages a faint smile. "Not as a meal. Remember when you were a child, how you liked to suck on anything sweet?" I swallow the inappropriate quip that I still do, and nod instead. "Our children picked up rocks and stones and sucked on those, dirt and all, every chance they got. They paid no attention to our hysteria about bacteria. We couldn't prevent them from doing it."

I have heard of a condition called pica, an abnormal appetite for nonfood substances such as paint or clay or dirt, but, remembering some of my own distinctive likes and dislikes around food as a child, I suggest, "A dietary deficiency? Or craving?"

She visibly stifles her impatience. "Exactly what we thought, Joss. I assure you, we ran every test. Dietary deficiency didn't explain it. So I guess we're left with craving." Her tone is sarcastic.

I nod apologetically. I'm sure everything that occurs to me—and many more theories to explain their baffling behavior besides the ones I can think of—has already undergone the most thorough investigation by our Unity.

"The changes in their sleeping patterns were just as inexplicable," Emerald tells me. "The way they slept, they resembled Earth cats. They curled up for long periods any hour of the day and night, and we'd find them everywhere—in trees, asleep on rocks, on the seaside moss, in grass, stretched out on plain soil—"

"In their homes?"

She shakes her head. "Everywhere but there."

"Even during the nocturnals?"

"Yes. Even then. They did what our animals do. As soon as the winds begin, all the animals get themselves inside any area of grass. And our grass grows everywhere on Femina—it's fully adapted to the winds. The outer perimeter lifts upright and becomes a sealed barrier. Our children did exactly the same as the animals."

I remember reading about this phenomenon from the accounts of the first landing on Maternas when Megan, Mother, and the Inner Circle were caught in the lethal nocturnal winds near the sea and followed a whoofie to safety in the grasses. Gazing at the women around me, the way their beautiful nude bodies move with easy grace and strength, I remark, "They seem indeed to have much in common with animals."

She nods. "The slightest noise would awaken them—just like cats. They'd sleep entwined together—just like kittens."

"But not sexually?"

"Oh, yes, sexually. Definitely sexual. Sometimes it was hard to tell," she says wryly. "They slept in groups and very much entwined, and were sexual very early on. How would they not be? As you can see they're all next to naked."

These women who are so close to my own age or younger—I am fascinated by their generational departure in behavior. Rebellion well beyond anything of my own experience or knowledge, beyond anything I would ever have dreamed. I cannot conceive of why so extreme a breaking off from the previous generations needed to occur. And, in view of this rejection, why they've made Emerald and me their captives—and what they intend to do with us.

I'm distracted by what has gradually emerged before us: a soaring wall. A wall of solid ivory-blue so daunting and impressive it might well be a tidal wave poised to swamp us.

"Are we going in there too?" Emerald asks apprehensively.

The wall appears to be solid. There is something significant about it: We are being pushed directly toward it with purpose and at a faster pace.

But as we approach, the wall acquires more definition. In shape it is more pyramid than wall, and I see natural footholds all over the graduated incline of its surface. Impossible as it seems, we will be walking up a vast hedge of foliage—the women ahead of us are already ascending in apparent eagerness, and ease. Another item of note: The rain has ceased.

Moving ahead of Emerald, I take the first step up. It's hard to imagine so solid a compacting of plant life, yet the elasticity of the footing tends to spring me up to the next level, and all around me women much larger than myself are scaling this pyramid with speed and confidence, all of them upright; the incline is much more hill than mountain.

"It may be underpinned with a rock formation," I tell Emerald, who has come bounding up the hill to be level with me.

"Hard to say," she replies, after gently probing the surface with the toe of her boot. "It's so spongy it could be compacted plant life."

For now we no longer speak; we're both occupied scaling our hill.

Perhaps, soon now, we will finally learn the reason why we have been brought here.

PERSONAL JOURNAL OF MINERVA

Though our decision has been made to land on Gearhart Island and proceed from there, the *Marie Curie* continues in a low flight pattern over Amazonia. We have no reason to make haste from where our loved ones have gone missing, other than gaining the possibility of extra sleep, which will be an elusive aspiration at best this night.

Overriding the natural cohesion of our Sisterhood and the loving protection and reverence for life it accords to any member of our Unity under all circumstances, a more personal anxiety is felt by each of us. Megan is of course focused on her daughter Emerald. Danya, who has made only the briefest of acquaintance with Joss, would also be far more concerned with Emerald. As for me, I knew Emerald as a little girl and retain a specific fondness for her because of my love for Megan and Emerald's association with those heady glory days when we first arrived here and created our colony of Cybele. But over recent years I have come to know Joss; to have as much regard and affection—let me say it, love—for this special young woman as Olympia feels toward her. I love her quiet strength and courage, the innate dignity she displayed throughout the tumultuous events on Earth and their aftermath—the fate that befell Africa Contrera. I see the inherent loneliness that Tara has tried in vain to quench.

All four of us scrutinize our instrument readings as if to will contact with Emerald and Joss, as if some sudden visual sighting will materialize from the precision sightings of our drones. Something—anything—to relieve our anxiety. The two suns of Maternas are falling toward the horizon line on this side of the continent, but infrared nighttime sensors will avail us nothing—the jungle below teems with life, human as well as animal, and we know that many other lost daughters of Maternas have taken up habitation in the area.

There is another development.

In our continuous communication with the Unity in Cybele throughout our venture, we have apprised them of the intention to land on Gearhart Island and proceed from there. In response, two contingents have departed from Cybele on the *Eleanor Roosevelt* and the *Margaret Mead*, the *Eleanor* team led by Diana and also by Venus, whose profession as biologist will undoubtedly stand us in good stead. The *Mead* group is headed by Hera, accompanied by Vesta, who successfully argued the necessity for having her psychological skills on hand, and Tara, of course. Both ships will carry the rest of Danya's security team, along with additional flitters. The plan is for all of us to reconnoiter on Gearhart Island, then employ every available flitter to venture to the Vanessa River and land there in numbers.

A message is just coming in from the *Mead*. Before I see the source, I know who it is from the illumination of joy in Olympia's face.

I have come to a few significant beliefs in my long life. One is that while we may fall in love with many, there is always someone who is the love of our life. Often it is our first love. For some it is our last love—such as myself, when I found my Christa. I also believe in what others term "grand design" or "natural balance," and I call the "wild card of chance." It was by only the sheerest good fortune I did not lose Christa when

I found her, when a death-dealing virus swept into Femina on spring winds during our first year on Maternas. To this day I tremble at the memory of when she lay in my arms at the brink of expiring, when she held on for those precious moments until Diana could arrive with the serum that separated loss of her from my years of happiness since.

Thus I know that Ceeley is the love of Olympia's life. And even though Ceeley withered in the relentless spotlight that comes with association with any member of the Inner Circle, and eventually fled from Olympia to the extent of making the journey to this world, I know that Olympia remains the love of Ceeley's life.

This emotional entanglement aside, Ceeley is also one of our meteorologists. Her quiet voice and ominous message fill the control room of the *Marie Curie:* "A cyclone is gathering strength a thousand miles off the coast of Gearhart Island."

Megan responds with the amazement we all feel: "That weather pattern was only forming when we took off."

"You're right, Megan. It's anomalous. But it's there. Fully aggregated and gathering momentum toward land."

"Yet another anomaly…" Megan turns to me, and there is bafflement, helplessness, despair in her green eyes. "Minerva," she implores me, "what is happening to our world?"

I am Minerva the historian; my powers extend to interpreting the past and recording the present, however I fervently I might long for it to be otherwise. "Megan, I wish I knew," I reply.

Megan visibly gathers herself. "Ceeley," she says in her usual tone of cool command, "what are the parameters?"

"Central pressure nine hundred and eighty-two millibars. Projection for Gearhart Island is scale five. Eight hundred kilometers in diameter and expanding, with current sustained winds of three hundred kilometers per hour."

A monster. Megan looks as shaken as I feel.

"Its ETA at Gearhart Island?"

"The front will arrive in four hours and nine minutes."

"Megan—" Danya begins, but Megan holds up a hand for silence as she considers this information and our options—which seem limited to one, in my view: abandon our plan.

"Hera," Megan says.

"Yes, Megan."

"Four hours puts all of us on Gearhart simultaneously only with the leading edge. We can make the transition to our flitters and leave before the full brunt hits. But we'll have to leave our three ships there. Can they be made secure?"

"Quite possibly," Hera responds with crisp authority. "If we land on the far side of the island and put the land mass between our ships and the storm."

Ceeley breaks in: "Large as it is, the storm may pick up even more force over the next hours, Megan."

"So there's a chance our ships may be destroyed."

"In that case," Hera replies, "more than a chance."

"Girls."

The identity of the new voice is unmistakable. The speaker is in Cybele, and she is the Mother of us all.

"Girls, get a move on. If your ships are destroyed, so be it. We'll just come and get you on Amazonia. Go get Emerald and Joss."

"Yes, Mother," Megan says with a grin. Squaring her shoulders, she issues her next command: "All ships, full speed for Gearhart Island."

PERSONAL JOURNAL OF JOSS

The top of the pyramid is vast, extending as far as the eye can see. Moments after sunset, in the darkening blue twilight, the landscape—strange to begin with, eerier territory if possible than the one from which Emerald and I have just ascended—is turning even more fantastic.

The area is astonishingly well-populated. I cannot estimate how many young women surround us, but many dozens mill within my view, and at least as many others undoubtedly are concealed amid the clusters of trees and foliage.

Even with a sort of woodland all around us, the "floor" beneath our feet is smooth yet spongy, and wildly uneven as if we walk over solidified waves, some as high as two meters.

Emerald, staring with a fascination equal to mine, jabs repeatedly at the ground. "Leaves," she exclaims, "it's all leaves, Joss!"

Indeed it is—unlike anything I have ever seen. The surface is richly patterned, an intricate leaf mosaic. The few leaves that lie intact and as yet covered by others are the size of those we saw growing at jungle level, and are in fact the same leaf species. Thus we have our first rational explanation for one aspect of the behavior of these women: why they collected them from the jungle floor. Several of those who brought us here are on hands and knees flattening and pressing the newly arrived leaves into place near where we stand.

Since I carry no instrument with a cutting edge, I test where we stand with the toe of my boot, then lean down to run a fingernail over it, increasing the pressure. The leaf under me remains unmarked, impervious. Malleable as it is underfoot, it is also extremely tough, and if there is perhaps little of actual substance beneath where we stand, it doesn't matter. The surface is efficient, versatile, uncomplicated, unique.

A strip of light, from one of our small glowing moons, emerges from a parting of the cloud cover to reveal variations of blue and gray hues in the mosaic, probably reflecting the age of the leaves—the newest are a brighter ivory-blue. If the surface is this spectacular in the moonlight of an intensifying night, it must be truly extraordinary in the light of day.

Many of the women around us sprawl unceremoniously in declivities on the surface, their nude bodies an aesthetic delight in their various states of repose. Many gaze off into the horizon as the final light of day extinguishes; some sit, leaning back into the waves. There seems little contact among them, except with their young whom they embrace and stroke with rough, artless affection; and everyone fluffs the fur of a number of whoofies that have somehow gotten themselves all the way to this continent—unless they were taken here or even perhaps originated here. No one, including the youngest children—including even the whoofies—displays the slightest interest in us.

"Adira!"

Emerald lunges over the uneven surface toward a dark-haired woman standing with her back to us. She seizes the woman's arm with both hands, whirls her around...and slumps in disappointment. Then quickly recovers to dash in among the women. I follow as best I can. If only I knew what her daughter looks like, I could assist. Still, Emerald is far from shy, jostling her way toward anyone who catches her eye amid the trees and foliage, increasingly frenzied, boldly seizing any dark-haired one so she can see her face. None of them appear to be startled. None of them show any reaction.

I suddenly glimpse young women *I* recognize. "Netis! Kaylee! Niabi!" I call out in great excitement to the magnificent young women I met when I first came to this world. I rush toward the daughters of my sister Trella's two daughters.

They do not seem to hear me. When I confront them directly I see in their eyes that they do know me—and are indifferent to that knowledge. Not exactly turning their backs on me, they move off casually, and even though I doggedly pursue them, they do not and will not turn or speak, ignoring my insistent presence as if I were an insect that did not rise to the level of annoyance. So thoroughly am I dismissed from their consciousness that I might not even exist.

I stomp away in a rage and in full agreement with the Sisterhood's frustration over this incomprehensible faction of our Unity. And manage to humiliate myself even further as each furious step on the springy surface propels me into the air like a bouncing ball. Fortunately, Emerald hasn't seen me, so I work at calming myself and assembling my remaining shreds of dignity.

In apparent realization of the futility of her own search, Emerald has returned, having made a wide circle of our area, evidently as unwilling as I am to go too far afield from where we came up to this plateau, lest we become even more lost than we already are. She slumps into a hollow, head between her knees, and runs her hands through her fine dark hair. I sit beside her but do not speak, leaving her to gather her composure.

"I'm so thirsty," she finally confesses in a whisper.

Now that we have arrived at what seems to be a final destination, so am I. With all the rain that's drenched us, we've not thought to drink any of it. I'm also very hungry—I have yet to eat a morsel on this planet. Thus far I have seen no one with any food or drink. But amid our futile pursuit of familiar faces I did notice irregular channels streaming with the recent rain and assume these must lead to a collection point.

I continue to be alert to what happens around us, but my adrenaline level has returned to near normal. Whatever purpose these women intend to make of us, whatever their reason for leading Emerald and me here, I feel even more confident that we are not destined to be anyone's meal.

A sound intrudes on my thoughts, faint yet penetrating and brief, something like a penetrating hum. A signal: The women have turned toward its origin to our left and move toward it as if under command. After an exchange of uneasy glances, Emerald and I get to our feet and follow. It seems as good an option as any.

Under a night sky streaked with thin clouds shot through with creamy greenish light from a star cluster of emerald and gold, we make our way across the uneven, pliant surface of the plateau as if we walk the deck of a ship at sea. Emerald seems unmoved by the splendor, but then she was born on this planet and perhaps has become inured to its nightly splendors. Besides, she has her own preoccupations.

We travel perhaps a hundred meters to an immense pool of water glistening in the glow of the firmament. A welcome sight indeed, especially in view of the dozens of women seated in clusters at its edge, some drinking water from cone-shaped containers, or from their cupped hands; others, especially the younger ones, lying on their stomachs and drinking as animals do. We rush toward the pool, flinging ourselves down on our knees beside it, caring nothing about any decorum, only that the water is lovely and obviously safe to drink.

And good. In fact delicious. Cool in my cupped hands, and so nectar-like that I continue to drink beyond the slaking of my thirst. I hadn't known that the water on this world could be so delectable.

"Is it me," Emerald asks between swallows, "or is this water sublime?"

"It's wonderful," I reply, disappointed that it is not naturally occurring and must contain some added ingredient. Hopefully, when—if—we get ourselves away from here, we'll be able to find this water elsewhere.

Intent on slaking our thirst, neither of us has noticed till now that the majority of our companions did not come here to drink but instead are gathered around a mound. We draw near, to discover the mound is composed of large, glowing, ivory-colored, flutelike flowers.

"They look like an oversize version of Earth's calla lilies," I murmur to Emerald, who nods uncomprehendingly—unsurprising, since she has never seen one. It's also evident these flowers provide the goblets employed by some of the women for scooping and drinking water out of the pool.

And that they are an eating staple as well. All the women are pulling what appear to be apples from them and consuming them. I lean closer. Each of the flowers in the mound holds in its heart a fruit or perhaps a large globular seed. Of uniform size, this food source is multicolored like a Fuji or gala apple, but when I pick one up it has the heft and dimpled surface of an orange and its skin seems to be more of a rind.

The flowers are arranged like a bouquet, interconnected to the extent that they are all standing straight up, stem down. The reason is apparent: Each flower contains liquid. Watching the women around me for clues, I see that they gather an assortment of four or five flowers, seat themselves in haphazard fashion, pluck out the fruit or whatever it is from within the flower, and eat it while sipping from the liquid remaining in the flute.

Shrugging, Emerald plucks a flower out of the mound. "I think we're meant to help ourselves," she remarks.

I nod but do not take one, instead looking at the mound of flowers more closely. In the dark blueness of this night, the glowing blooms are varied shades of ivory, and the fruit has all different hues as well, corals, yellows, blues, as does the interior of each flower, and the liquid inside, although in this light I cannot determine what all those hues might be. It's an exquisite sight, this mound of strange moonlit flowers, and as I lift my gaze I see there are other mounds in addition to this one, extending to who knows where. Perhaps to where they were harvested.

Now to taste. I choose a flower, one with a comparatively light-colored interior, and pluck the fruit from its nest. There is no resistance. Indeed there seems no connection between it and its host, no stem, no tendrils to feed sustenance to it from its host flower and the tree or bush that bore it. Unless the laws of nature do not apply on this world, it must absorb nutrients in some other way. But as I inspect the surface, I cannot see how.

"Joss," Emerald says, and there is something in her tone that draws my instant attention.

"Joss," Emerald says again, and she has consumed half of her fruit and her eyes are closed, and the tone is one of rapture.

I bite through a rind, thin, tasting faintly, delicately, of citrus. The next texture is crispness, like an apple. But no apple ever dazzled my taste buds with such flavors: vanilla and mango and honey. I eagerly take more bites. No seeds, no core. It is the most delicious food I have ever had in my mouth, and I have been fortunate enough in my life to have had meals at Vesta's table. I finish the fruit quickly, greedily, knowing there are more, many more available to us, and then tip up the flower to drink its liquid. And taste ambrosia.

"Yes," I dreamily reply to Emerald, still savoring the peach-cinnamon aftertaste. She is consuming the flower in its entirety, as are other women around us. As do I. My ivory flute dissolves into nothingness on my tongue, leaving behind shaded flavors of cocoa.

Eager to experience again these incredible tastes and textures, Emerald and I choose another blossom. Mine this time is the shade of alabaster, with a darker interior and holding a fruit with a slightly different coloration from the one I've just devoured. The texture this time is creamy, not crisp, and the taste is a combination of pecan and pear. The liquid is lemony; the flower tastes of almond.

Emerald chooses four more, arranging and holding them like a bouquet. "Let's sit over there," she says, indicating a wave in the surface with a high back to its curve. I select four blooms of my own and accompany her.

Where we sit serves as a bench, and a most comfortable one at that with its malleable seat and back, a place where we can linger and exclaim over the delights of the most exotic food either of us has eaten.

We pass our food back and forth, and soon discover no two items are alike in texture, ranging from the softness of ice cream and sponge-like oranges to the crunchy firmness of jicama to the chewiness of seeds, of licorice. The tastes are even more varied—nutlike, spicy, every variation of fruit. The flower as well—the flavors are of exotic teas, of honeyed chocolate. And the liquid within the flower—I taste passion fruit, sweet milk, berries.

"I didn't know anything like this existed on our planet," Emerald tells me.

How could the Unity not know? I wonder.

As if she has heard my thought, she continues, "For decades entire professions in our Unity were dedicated to thorough exploration and assessment of our planet. But where we go is subject to strict provisions of our charter. Whole areas remain unexplored except for surveillance and measurements from altitude no matter how enticing they may be. We enter no territory where we could do any damage to the land—like this one: a pure wilderness where landing a craft could destroy habitats."

I hear this explanation with both admiration for its high moral principle and misgiving for its applied practicalities. Adhering to such a philosophy will substantially cut the chances for our rescue by the Unity. Where, aside from the rock where the *Sarah Bernhardt* sits disabled, could a rescue party land anywhere close to us?

But I do not voice my thought.

PERSONAL JOURNAL OF OLYMPIA

We are closing in on Gearhart Island, only twenty minutes away. Ceeley, onboard the *Margaret Mead,* has been updating us minute to minute on the weather status at the island. Her reports are ominous.

Unknowable dangers lie ahead, I tell myself. Our worsening circumstances may conspire to separate us again, this time permanently. "Ceeley," I say impulsively. I am not on view and glad for it, since I sit in confusion: I've not given a thought as to what I should now say in these most public of circumstances. I take refuge in the obvious: "It appears the closer we come to the island, the more the typhoon picks up speed."

"Olympia," Ceeley replies gently. Then, addressing the crisis at hand and my stupidly obvious comment: "So rapid an increase in speed over water is unprecedented. An anomaly."

Everything occurring on this planet seems to be an anomaly. And to my untutored eyes, a pattern of menace. But her voice is like a caress, and beyond that, a comfort. As is my sister Minerva's hand on my arm and her smile. Minerva has always known of my true feeling for Ceeley.

"Esteemed Hera," Danya says, eyes narrowed as she scrutinizes her readings, "status?"

"It will be close," Hera replies tersely from the *Margaret Mead*. "With such uncertainty whether we can get our flitters off the island in time we must reconsider our—"

"Megan." It is Diana, from the *Eleanor*. "Your orders?"

Thank you, Diana! I want to shout. Megan is in command here, for reasons that have been famously demonstrated throughout our history.

"Hera, I understand and have assessed your concerns. All ships will remain on course to land on Gearhart Island," Megan instructs from beside us in her clear, bell-like tones. "Recheck every procedure for immediately disembarking. All ships will land ninety degrees east into the wind. Under no circumstances will tethering commands consume more than ten seconds. If landing conditions require additional computations, you are instructed to abandon ship."

The groan I hear is from Hera. Danya is grimacing. No pilot of any ship wishes to hear such an order.

"No exceptions," Megan states, with a stern glance at Danya. "Not even one second. Am I clear?"

A chorus of "Yes, Megan."

"Are all flitters in place for takeoff from the rear of each ship?"

Another chorus of "Yes, Megan."

"For maximum protection all flitters will take off ninety degrees due west directionally with the wind until well clear. Understood?"

Yet another chorus of "Yes, Megan."

Beneath us now is a dark, awe-inspiring, daunting, terrifying sight, and we are dropping rapidly from a royal-blue star-shimmering sky into a massive maw churning with black clouds and lightning-shot turbulence.

"All hands, check your restraints," Megan orders, her emerald gaze fixed on the dimensional readings of the monster we face.

No need to persuade any of us. As the first winds reach us

and our craft begins to roll and then sharply buck, Minerva clasps my hand and I hold hers tightly and close my eyes, trusting my fate to the judgment of Megan and the superb piloting skills of Danya.

But I open them again. If my life is to end, then of what use is cowering? I refuse to have the end come with my eyes closed.

The *Marie Curie* shudders violently as if with fever, and I watch Danya fight to hold her level, calibrating and recalibrating as our craft bores into winds of such force that they act as their own braking device as we descend, descend, descend.

We thud and thump to a landing, and Danya is already keying in a series of commands, all the while pleading, "Come on, *Marie,* come on…"

"All hands to the flitters," Megan commands. "*Now.*"

Danya leaps to her feet and slams a hand on the control console of the *Marie Curie* and yells, "Good girl!"

From this I trust all has been made secure—assuming these inconceivable winds do not, despite Danya's efforts, wrench our faithful craft loose from her tethering and fling her into the far reaches of the ocean.

As the rear panels open, I halt, mesmerized. Unbelievable sound—an elemental, earsplitting scream of raging wind lifts the hair on the back of my neck. Then equally unbelievable sight—rain like multiple horizontal waterfalls and with it uprooted trees flung like arrows, some of them smiting the *Marie Curie.* If I were to step out onto the surface of Gearhart Island, I could not breathe in the wetness, and my robe, no matter how sodden with rain, would balloon out from my body and become a sail, hoisting me from the ground and propelling me higher and higher into the stratosphere.

The strong hands of Megan and Danya pull me out of my nightmarish reverie, yanking and dragging me along and then unceremoniously shoving me in a tumble into the confines of our flitter. My ears hurt from the sudden quiet. And from Minerva raging about the intellectual deficiencies of a sister who would consider stopping to gaze at a typhoon a good idea.

Danya hastily unlocks the flitter mooring and floats it out of the *Marie Curie,* and we instantly become a tumbling seed on the wind, flung along out of control and menaced on all sides by flying missiles.

"Full speed, all craft, full speed!" Megan orders.

It appears insane to add even more velocity to what seems an already suicidal track in our careening craft, but then I understand Megan's strategy: to outrun the leading edge of this storm. There is far less danger in trusting to instruments that will dodge objects in front of us than risk being overtaken and struck and fatally crippled by objects from behind.

As we careen along I can only wonder if all my sisters are with us, if Ceeley.... But the priority for us all is to escape from what pursues us, and Megan maintains transmission silence.

Finally, finally, our flitter begins to stablize, and Danya assumes manual control.

Megan speaks: "All craft, report."

"Here, Megan." It is Diana. I do not comprehend the names of the three women in her flitter, only that none of them is Ceeley.

"Here, Megan." Venus. None of the three in her craft are Ceeley.

"Here, Megan," says Vesta, "along with Haritha and Rida."

Other flitters report in—Danya's security team.

Nothing from Hera. And Tara and Ceeley are with Hera.

Their craft is missing.

PERSONAL JOURNAL OF JOSS

I seem to have lost track of time, my chronometer having suffered the same fate as my inoperative E-band. All I know is that in the radiance of the celestial splendor above us the woman sitting across from me is captivating, her face framed by tousled hair of ebony black, her eyes an exact match for the emerald hue in the nebula low on the horizon behind her slim shoulders. Amid her almost playful pleasure in the food we consume, Emerald has lost awareness of her sorrow and of the uncertainty of our circumstances; her supple body has assumed lovely, easy postures of relaxation.

A delicious lassitude has spread over my limbs, so much so that I find myself in an uncharacteristic, quite undignified sprawl, leaning back on my elbows with my legs splayed. My sense of well-being may have something to do with what we are consuming. Gazing into the flower flute from which I sip, I wonder whether its intoxicating flavor is more than metaphorical. A line from a twentieth-century woman poet floats through my mind, something about a bee drunk on dew. We know nothing of the food here, whether these women assimilate it differently or have acquired tolerance for its properties. *Whether*—this occurs to me with a stirring of disquiet—*it is perhaps a factor in the strangeness of their behavior.*

I have been intoxicated once in my life, in the controlled circumstance of being with a close friend, both of us having wanted to experience the sensations; I do not now feel that same heedlessness or any similar loss of inhibition or command. Surely not the diminution of my shyness. That particular flaw, along with all my perceptions and senses, seems undiminished.

If anything, my senses have heightened—and sharpened in most considerable dimension. The fragrances of this place provide their own intoxicant: jasmine-like scents on the gentle breezes of a tropical night, the loaminess rising from the leafy floor and the profligate foliage around us, the fusion of smells from the mounds of warm, edible flowers. And, wafting its subtle, insistent way to me, the ineffably sensual fragrance arising from Emerald's skin, the scents of musk, of woman...

The night air is an entity that bathes my face, caresses my skin...I have never been so easy with my body that I could display it, but now it feels imprisoned in its clothing, and I long to strip it off, to join the women around me, to feel the tender air palpate every surface of me. I stroke the ductile leaves on which I recline...they are burnished silk under my palm. Even my hearing is inundated, with the whisper of leaves in the trees and shrubs, the faint fluttering of the fabric of Emerald's shirt in the soft equatorial breezes of this glorious night.

My vision is of such clarity that I can see every particular in the leafy mosaic on which we recline, every ruffle on its surface, every nuance of its veins, the coloration of every slant of starlight and moonlight. The delicate silk in the hollow of Emerald's throat inhabits my senses so acutely I might be stroking it with my fingertips. With my tongue...

Desire for her is a filigree that has long since settled itself across all other sensory perceptions. Desire I will not act on. Even in these precarious circumstances anything between us must be initiated by her, not me. I wonder what will happen as this night deepens.

"How do these women sleep?" Emerald asks languorously. She sits looking at me, a hand clasped around one raised knee, her head back against the wave against which she rests. "*Where* do they sleep? How about us? Where will we sleep?"

What would be wrong with right here with you, I think, but before I can reply, six women approach.

One, a powerful-looking young woman with tawny skin, holds out a hand to Emerald. With a look of wonderment, Emerald unhesitatingly takes the hand and allows herself to be lifted to her feet. I begin to scramble to my own feet but a gentle push by one of the others restores me unceremoniously to my sitting position.

Hand in hand with the woman, Emerald allows herself to be led away, accompanied by two others. Again I attempt to rise, with the same result. "Emerald, wait!" I shout.

She halts abruptly, as if jolted from a trance, then turns to me. Takes in my situation. Then she simply turns around walks away from me with her three companions. I scarcely believe my eyes. How can she want us to be separated?

I struggle more forcefully to get up. And yet again am pushed down.

"Emerald!" I scream. "Don't go with them!"

Again she stops. "Joss," she calls, "they may be taking me to my daughter."

"You don't know that!"

"Neither do you. I have to do this, Joss."

"Then make them take me too," I insist.

"If they wanted that, they'd allow it," she replies. "Joss, don't worry. I can take care of myself." She moves off, shoulders squared, her body conveying stubborn finality.

I can offer no further argument. I watch Emerald until the ice blue of her shirt is swallowed up in the gloom. Then I slump down and cross my arms over my raised knees, prepared to wait as long as it takes these women to leave so I can get up and search for her. I do not feel tired—my senses are too wide open for that—and it would not matter if I did. I will not sleep until I find Emerald, or she returns.

The three who prevented me from following her continue to hover over me. After a time I look up at them, wondering why they're still here. To my surprise, they seat themselves before me. The one in the center, a dark-haired woman with full lips and voluptuous breasts, kneels before me, sitting back on her heels in a pose that under other circumstances would be breathtaking—her body is of such curving perfection that she might be a goddess.

The women here have initiated no physical contact except the one who extended her hand to Emerald and led her away. And they have yet to address a word to us. Nothing to be lost in trying again, I tell myself, and I address the goddess in front of me: "Where are they taking her?"

She does not speak, but her coral eyes meet mine and are mesmerizing, sending a beam of heat into the core of me. She reaches to me, brushes a tendril of hair from my forehead. I sit perfectly still, held in her gaze, electrified with surprise—and awareness. The band these women usually wear under their breasts is gone. Even though it is so small a thing to remove, it seems hugely symbolic, and to my eyes the three sitting before me seem newly and shockingly nude.

The woman to my left, slender, dark-haired, her almond skin as glossy as lustervel, reaches to me and takes my hand; long, pliant fingers curl caressingly around mine. The one to my right, her white-blond hair illuminated by moonlight, takes my other hand; she too entwines her fingers with mine.

Astonishing as these events are, I am more amazed by a sound. One I have not heard before either on this world or on my previous one, or perhaps have never been able to hear until now, when my senses seem so open, exposed, vulnerable. The sound is scarcely audible yet rises from all around me, like a hum, but not a hum, something more subtle, yet engulfing: I feel it as a tremor in my throat, flowing over my breasts and down my arms and legs. I glance away to ascertain its source—and then my attention is wrenched back to something inconceivable: soft, smooth hands on my shoulders. My bare shoulders. Again I am held, heated by a gaze of purest coral.

Loss of consciousness? Hypnotic trance? It must be one of these; I have no memory of how I have become as naked as the women who surround me.

Transfixed, I continue to stare into the coral eyes of the woman kneeling before me even as her hands glide down from my shoulders. My own hands are still held by the women on either side of me. and I could not move if I wanted to, and I have no will to do so as my breasts are clasped, and slowly, sensuously explored. She still does not take her gaze from mine and I cannot look away from her as I feel her hands with the most acute pleasure, the texture of her palms, the slow slide of them, the shape and curving of her long fingers as she cradles, enfolds, rolls the flesh of my breasts within her hands. A fingertip grazes my nipples and as each separate fingertip in turn caresses them they become hot filaments of pleasure. I can barely breathe.

Her coral eyes seem to grow larger as she leans toward me, ever closer, and then I must close my own eyes as her arms reach for me, slide around me, and my aching nipples are brushed by her full warm breasts, and she presses their luxuriant softness into me, nestles them into my breasts, and then molds her silken body to mine. She lowers me. Again I can barely breathe; every molecule of my being has opened to receive the richness of her magnificent body. And still the other two women hold my hands, their fingertips caressing my palms...

Her breath touches me and softly bathes one ear and then the other, and I writhe helplessly into her. Her lips touch me, a pillowy opulence beneath my ear, moving down over my throat...I arch with the first stroke of her tongue in the hollow of my throat, and again, and with every stroke that follows.

She lifts her body from mine, a void that is filled when her hands clasp my breasts and her lips return to my body, under my breasts, moving across and then down.

Impossibly, at the same time her mouth moves down me my nipples are enclosed in exquisite warmth. I open my eyes to see that is the lips of the women on either side of me that have taken possession of my breasts.

Hands stroke my hair, fingertips graze my shoulders, my throat—whose I do not know. Again I close my eyes as my nipples throb with nearly unendurable pleasure, as hands begin caressing within my willing thighs, spreading them fully. I shudder uncontrollably as a hand cups me, as fingers begin a light stroking between my legs, in arousal so fierce and so complete my body rocks, quickly gathers, surges into orgasm.

The tongues stroking my nipples do not stop; between my legs fingers slide along my wetness and sink deeply into me; a tongue opens the wet lips between my legs. I hear that sound again, and it is more than sound; it now palpably invades me. It is sound and vibration, and the vibration is in the tongues on my nipples, vibration is in the fingers within me, vibration is in the stroking tongue between my legs. Incandescent with sensation, a quivering tension of ecstasy, my body fuses into phase upon phase of orgasm. In the first ebbing I open my eyes and my body could be the nebula spread in a glorious red-blue-gold spectacle over my head.

It does not end. I am seated on a edge of a wave. Is this a dream? If so it is the dream of all dreams.

The slender, almond-skinned woman now stands below where I sit. She spreads my legs once again, spreads the lips within my legs with her fingertips, then eases her hips between my thighs. I feel a slight, malleable protuberance, feel it fitted perfectly against the source, the heart of my pleasure. She takes me in her arms and holds me to her, and

I hear the sound again and feel her vibration between my legs and in my breasts. I am spent, incapable of further arousal. I take her face in my hands to look at her, and her eyes are fixed on me as if she is looking into my depths. The vibration continues and continues, and pleasure ignites, and from there rapidly intensifies until I gasp, and the woman slides her hands under my knees and lifts my legs and begins a rhythmic surging into me, merging her own pleasure with mine. I thrash with my sensations the vibration increases, invades me, spreading up my stomach and with it comes the first pulse of my orgasm, combining with the powerful pulsing of hers…

At the very height of orgasm I hear something inside me. Not within my ears but somewhere deeper. It is not words. It is meaning, faint but specific meaning:

ALL OF YOU…

I cannot sense the rest of it; it ebbs with my own ebbing. Gently, the woman lowers my legs and eases herself away from me.

The blond woman takes her place. As she too fits herself precisely to me, I am still vibrating in the aftermath from the one before and the vibration renews with her and she slides her hands under my hips and presses me fully into her. Then she begins a slow rotation of my hips, gazing at me as if she too sees into me and, beyond that, senses my every pleasure, and she takes me with increasing urgency, heightening each rising sensation with avid rotations of her own hips.

At the peak of our orgasms the words that are not words come to me again:

ALL OF YOU
MUST LE…

I cannot comprehend the next word before the ebbing takes it from me.

The first woman to touch me has come to me again, and this time I understand what has to happen and I reach for her and this time she gives me her spectacular body to savor as I surrender my own to hers, wrapping my legs around her, pressing up into her, knowing where she must take me again, abandoning myself to however it is she will take me there. An unknowable time later, at the height of ecstasy, the words that come to me are:

ALL OF YOU
MUST LEAVE

PERSONAL JOURNAL OF MINERVA

As I awaken, I am groggily aware that Olympia is asleep beside me and that someone has lowered our chair backs while we slept. I can tell by the positions of the suns over the horizon line that it is only an hour or so after dawn. Having experienced the very heights of terror in fleeing the typhoon, the moment our flitters found a blessedly pacific stretch of weather, Olympia and I succumbed to our exhaustion, to our anxiety over the missing Hera and Ceeley and Tara, and slept where we sat. Now we soar over a vast area of heaving coral ocean, its waves flashing brilliantly under our suns. I awaken my deeply sleeping sister.

"Any word?" Olympia immediately asks, sitting up as if her body is on a spring but rubbing her hands over her tired face.

Danya shakes her head.

"Hera is most resourceful," Megan says.

She looks drawn. For obvious reasons. She has returned to this world and been reunited with Laurel, only to suffer news of loss, and now more loss, the disappearance of their daughter. And it was Megan's order that overrode Hera's judgment that we should abort the plan to land on Gearhart Island. So not only does Megan have a daughter missing, her sister Tara—Joss's lover—is now on that same list of the missing.

If it turns out that my sister is safe, I will never say another cross word to her, no matter how provocative or arrogant she may be. What Megan says about Hera's resourcefulness is indisputably true, but I am not foolish enough to believe that in the face of a cataclysmic typhoon, resourcefulness is anything but a commodity of distinctly limited value.

We approach Amazonia, our six craft in close formation. In silence we consume energy bars and sweet tea while we descend, closing in on our tiny landing site on the Vanessa River. Our suns have long since been obscured by layered clouds, and we are being pulled into heavy weather; it so buffets our tiny craft that Olympia and I clutch each other in the echoing fear of last night. Megan orders more distance between each craft.

Wind and rain would not be so much as a nuisance to a rugged ship like the *Sarah Bernhardt,* nor to the three others abandoned to their fate on Gearhart Island, but our flitters are fragile bubbles by comparison, designed for utilitarian transport duties on our continent of Femina. Their weight-bearing and power capacities have been stretched to the utmost by our improvised plan to quickly mount a rescue operation for Emerald and Joss. Thus far that plan has not been a sterling success. Now we face the risk of having to land our six little ships in pounding rain on an area whose size dictates the necessity for pinpoint precision.

"All craft," Megan says quietly. "This will be our landing plan. Assume a straight-line flying pattern on the Vanessa River, in the flight order to be assigned to you by Danya, this craft being last. On landing, you are to anchor in closest proximity to the *Sarah Bernhardt* to allow maximum clearance for the rest of us. Am I clear? Any questions?"

What is clear is that as the last craft, ours will be left with the minimum landing area and the maximum danger.

"Megan." The speaker is Vesta. "Your instructions are clear and will be followed to the letter except that I must insist you land first, not last."

Before Megan can respond, Danya interrupts. "Esteemed Vesta, I can land this little ship on the palm of your hand."

I'm sure she can; the controls of our craft are dwarfed in her large, capable hands.

"I have no doubt of your skills," Vesta returns in her sweet tones, "but this goes beyond your abilities to what is in everyone's best interest. Megan is our leader."

"Esteemed Vesta, I agree," Danya says immediately.

"Vesta—"

"Vesta is correct." The voice interrupting Megan comes to us from Femina. "Megan, you will be first to land."

"Yes, Mother," Megan says resignedly. "Proceed, Danya."

Mother has made no mention of the newly missing. Not even to issue her usual overconfident "I'm sure you girls can manage." From this can be gauged her level of concern and distress.

Brief minutes later we swoop down through curtains of gray rain, virtually skimming the surface of the churning Vanessa River. Our craft dips lower still, we swerve sharply left, and my stomach feels as if it has plummeted to the floor. I am Minerva the historian, I remind myself. I am duty bound not to close my eyes.

We brake with sickening abruptness into a rocking hover, then Danya sets us down in a feather-light if wobbly landing. I hear an explosive sigh of relief from someone, somewhere—possibly me. Then Danya taxis roughly over the rock, onto an edge so slanting that our craft teeters over the river.

"Flitter two, you are clear to land," Megan says calmly. "We are secure."

Secure? We have landed, but in my eyes are hardly secure. Assessing the choice of drowning in thunderous rain or remaining in a craft that may topple into the thrashing river, I clamber out into the elements, Olympia following with alacrity.

Soaked in heavy, gray curtains of rain we watch our flitters coming in one by one for precarious landings, then cradling themselves so close to the *Sarah Bernhardt* they could be the suckling offspring of a mother ship.

We are finally here, twenty of us. Except for our missing three.

The next priority requires no command from Megan, and she in fact leads the rush toward the *Sarah Bernhardt*. I scurry to keep up with Megan's loping strides toward this first direct connection to the disappearance of her daughter, all of us hoping to find Emerald and Joss within.

We don't.

Since the ship's beacon is inoperative, the logical expectation is that we will not find a ship in navigable working order.

But we do. The ship is intact. No equipment is missing or damaged.

"All flight systems are operative," Danya reports to Megan.

"But not the beacon."

"No. Nor communications."

Something has happened here to prevent Joss and Emerald from transmitting their position or situation to us.

"They left the ship expecting to return," Danya says buoyantly. "They're probably lost and we just need to go find them."

"We can surmise they did not go far," Megan says, her voice bleak.

No one has to explain her reaction. Emerald and Joss came here for one reason only: for Emerald to find some closure to her grief by returning to the place where Danya had first brought her, where she found her dying daughter. That she had previously carried Esme back here, and that Emerald, slender of form, has limited endurance, means she found Esme quite close, within the radius where carrying an adult daughter would be a physical possibility. Why would Joss and Emerald venture any farther into an unexplored, forbidding continent deemed off limits to our Unity?

"Megan," Danya says, "if you recall, I told you she insisted on going in by herself but I can show you the direction where she went."

"I'll accompany you," I tell them. "I am Minerva—"

"The historian," Danya finishes grinning at me. "Of course you'll accompany us. We need to set our E-bands—" Danya breaks off, looking at her wrist in astonishment. "My E-band, communicator—"

"Neither is mine," I exclaim, shaking my wrist. "How can that be?"

"Were they operative when you were here before?" Megan inquires of Danya, her eyes narrowed.

"Of course," Danya says indignantly. "Do you think I'd allow your daughter—"

"Did you check?"

"*Did I check?* How can you—"

"In Hera's absence," Olympia says, in an attempt to bring some lightness into the bristling between Danya and Megan, "I'll suggest an anomalous electromagnetic interference has formed here."

Danya takes her charge rod from her belt, aims it down at the rock. "Operative," she says tersely.

"My apologies," Megan says stiffly. "Electromagnetic forces actually could be at work here. Affecting some equipment functions and not others."

Joss and Emerald would not have had charge rods. If they ventured into this jungle without the protection of their E-bands...I look up to meet Olympia's eyes and see the same fear in her.

"We'll proceed with charge rods and my entire security team," Danya states. "Everyone else is to remain here."

"Agreed," Megan says.

At a signal from Danya, a dozen burly women flank us, their presence an immediate buttress to my spirits.

Danya, her pants and shirt plastered by rain to her thick

frame, climbs down from the rock with our row of awkward drenched ducks following her, and leads us into a channel at river level. From the frying pan into the fire, as Mother would say. Or more appropriately, out of the rain, into the bedlam. I am so inundated by the screams of wildlife, so afflicted with claustrophobia that I stumble along aware only that I am miserably unqualified for the work of a historian. I am deafened and so filled with apprehension that we will be attacked momentarily by any manner of huge animal that I am able to record nothing beyond these purely visceral reactions.

Blessedly, we come to a sort of clearing, and I do my best to recover my wits without fainting on the spot. "They were here. Two people sat right there," Danya says, indicating a flattened pattern in the grass in front of a tree as she also consults a gauge on her enviro-reader. "I'm picking up numerous DNA readings, Megan. These are the strongest correlation to Emerald."

Megan sits in one of the flattened patterns, closing her eyes as if using her body as a divining rod for her daughter's presence. We remain silent; Danya continues to inspect the site.

Looking around her, Megan spots a disturbed pattern in the leaves on the jungle floor and brushes at it. She pulls at something she has found, then, her face stricken, she holds up a fine chain. I recognize it: It is the chain Megan placed around Emerald's neck when she was born.

She holds it in her palm for a time, then restores it to its place. "She placed it here for a reason, and did not mean for it to be found," she says quietly, brushing leaves back over the chain.

Danya continues to inspect the periphery of the seemingly impenetrable jungle. "In order to proceed, we will need to remain together for safety—our communicators are inoperative. The density is such that we will need to cut a swath."

This, of course, will bring an unknown toll of destruction to this jungle habitat and its inhabitants.

"We cannot proceed," Megan says with finality. "We'll return to our base. And reconnoiter."

It is the only possible decision. While hardly eager to reenter the corridor leading back to the rain, I am less eager for the alternative—entering that impossible jungle.

The question now is, what can we conceivably do from here? The weather would seem to preclude aerial reconnaissance of any value by our flitters. Why would tomorrow be different in a rain forest environment?

The possibility of finding Emerald and Joss seems sharply diminished. If not futile.

JOURNAL OF JOSS

ALL OF YOU MUST LEAVE

As an edge of coral dawn lightens the deep-blue horizon line, I sit back against the curve of a wave and continue to mull over this night and the message transmitted to me in what must surely be the most extraordinary new method of delivery since the invention of the telegraph.

What entity has passed me this message? Where is the message from? Collectively from these mute young women who have so determinedly removed their presence from our Unity? From a designated leader—perhaps the goddess-like woman of the night? A rational answer eludes me.

Where have we been told we "must leave" *from*? Cybele? Femina? Maternas? Does "all of you" apply to our entire Unity? Beyond all else, *why* is it that we "must leave"?

I have been given this message—entrusted with it—but what am I to do with it? How am I supposed to find my way from this place to deliver it?

As the sky brightens, clusters of women and children near me, slumbering in tangled embrace like litters of kittens, are stirring, pulling apart, awakening sluggishly. I myself feel refreshed. The women of the night, having taken me to sexual heights beyond imagination, afterward had each touched my forehead with her lips and left me, and I fell instantly and deeply into sleep, a sleep unique for me—sweet, intense, filled with kaleidoscopic dreams I cannot remember. Could this entire night have been a dream? A delirious orgasmic fantasy brought on by those exotic flowers we consumed?

"Joss."

I nearly leap with shock. There is mirroring surprise on Emerald's face and in her tone: "Where are your clothes?"

A glance down confirms I indeed am still naked. She, of course, wears her pants and shirt. I wonder, *Was she given the same message as I was by the three women who separated her from me? In the same way?* "Around somewhere," I reply to her question, gesturing vaguely, having no memory of where my clothes might be. "Are you all right?" I inquire, carefully inspecting her.

She looks at me with curiosity, puzzlement—and also in frank evaluation of my nakedness. "Yes, I'm all right."

After my abandonment to the pleasures lavished on me by three extraordinary women, I am no longer concerned with my previous notions of modesty. Although I wonder if the extent of their attentions shows on my body; my nipples, my pubis echo with a tender, sweet aching. "Where did they take you?" I ask.

She shrugs. "On some meandering route to nowhere. They finally let me go and just wandered off, each in a different direction. It was dark. I had no idea where I was, so I curled up and tried to sleep. They came back a while ago and brought me here." She adds in frustration, "Nothing they do makes any sense!"

But something is clear: The message was delivered only to me.

"What about you?" she says. "What happened here, Joss? Why did you take off your clothes?"

I choose the second question to answer and offer a version of the truth: "I felt very warm last night."

"Not me. I slept under one of those big leaves." She continues to look at me curiously. "You look...different," she says.

Uncertain what I should reveal to her, I temporize, "How so?"

"I'm not sure. You just seem different. A good many in our Unity wear next to nothing—but it just seems...somehow unlike you, Joss. From what I sense about you," she amends awkwardly.

She's right. I walk up one of the higher waves and spot my shirt and pants in a heap a short distance away, fetch them, and pull them on. Then I rejoin her where she now sits.

Making no acknowledgment of my more customary state, she veers onto a new topic: "I could hardly sleep for the noise."

"Noise?" Surely not from these silent women. Did I... "What kind of noise?"

"Joss, you *must* have heard it. A hum. Like purring. As if this whole place were filled with purring jungle cats." Again she stares at me in bewilderment. "You didn't hear the noise they make during their coupling?"

"That. Yes, I heard it," I say.

"I would think so. They were all around me, everywhere. All night long. Didn't you think it was really strange?"

"Maybe...maybe I didn't hear it quite as much or in the same way you did," I say distractedly. The high-intensity vibration that so keenly escalated the ecstasies of the night—could it be so simple as the purring mechanism of a cat? There was something entirely catlike about the three women in their unrestrained carnality and unselfconscious grace and beauty...I gaze at the females around me, some of them at the pond languidly drinking, some still in a somnolent curl as if reluctant to wake. There is something very catlike in all the women here, I realize.

"Are you hungry?"

"No," I say in surprise.

"Neither am I and I can't understand it. I wonder about those flowers we ate."

"So do I."

With the dawn has come heavy, deep coral clouds, and rain begins, an initial spatter of large heavy drops rapidly intensifying into a drenching downpour.

Her clothes and hair plastered to her, Emerald says in displeasure, "I wonder if it rains this hard every day."

The nature of the environment affirms that it does, that this is a rain forest. The concealment by clouds of the brilliant double suns and preternatural light of this alien world continue to be most welcome to me, aiding my assimilation. The day is already becoming oppressively warm. Right now I want to take the same advantage of the rain as the women around me. I fling off the clothes I have just donned and stand with legs apart, arms up, raising my face to the warm teeming rain, letting it stream down me, bathing my body and face, drinking it in, luxuriating in it.

"It's lovely," Emerald concedes from beside me. She has stripped nude to do the same. "You were right to take your clothes off, Joss," she says, kicking hers aside. "Why bother with them?"

My sexual desire sated—extinguished—by the exertions of the night, I gaze at her slender form streaming and gleaming with rain, and speak the truth: "You are truly beautiful."

"As are you, Joss. Your body—you could be an athlete. Your eyes..." She does not finish.

My body has never seemed to me anything more than sturdily functional, and my gray-blue eyes are not remotely comparable to the pure jewel-like emerald of hers...still, why argue with her generosity of view? "Thank you," I tell her.

I am just beginning to wonder what this new day will bring when the young women give us an unmistakable indication:

They are donning their breast bands and moving away from us en masse and with purpose. We hasten to follow.

As we walk across the plateau in the teeming rain, Emerald reaches for my hand. We may be lost here, but I don't feel it quite as much, not with her hand clasped firmly in mine.

I know several things now. If logic prevails, because I have been entrusted with a message, we will not be harmed. And we need to be taken somewhere so that I can deliver the message. And I know we are traveling in the opposite direction from our ship.

I continue to reflect over disclosing to Emerald the mysterious message I carry and how it was given to me—and her possible reaction if I do this. If someone I had known for two days came to me with a tale about words imparted in disjointed fashion at the height of the last three of six orgasms during a night filled with aggressive sexual congress with three women, how would I assess her view of reality?

Truthfully, I cannot explain it even to my own satisfaction. Telepathy does not account for the nature of what happened. If there had been such a process at work, and since thought travels faster than the speed of light, why would I not have received the entire message in the flash of an instant?

The essential question is, will my telling her any of this detract from or add to her comfort in being with me, her anxiety about what has happened to us? My judgment and intuition tell me that right now I should say nothing.

In teeming rainfall, as we follow the group to perhaps a kilometer beyond where we started, I glance at all the silent women we accompany but recognize none of them from the night. We have begun a gradual descent, and our footfalls land among small ferns, then in ferns that grow knee high. We are both barefoot, and like me Emerald seems to trust that since everyone around us is similarly exposed, whatever life-forms we might disturb within the ferns will not harm us.

We gradually move down into a jungle that appears identical

to the wiry, impenetrable tangle near the ship on the other side of our pyramid-plateau; certainly it is equally warm and humid here as it was there. But its appearance from a distance is deceiving; at ground level the density is much less, the trees farther apart and growing to a uniform ten-meter height, their tall, bushy crowns a massed aggregation jostling for a share of the light and giving the impression to any of the Unity's drones that the jungle beneath is impenetrable. Ground here is actually visible in many places, a rich deep coral where it lies bare of foliage, and there is only a sparse covering of fern at best on terrain so deeply shadowed that it might be evening here, both sun and rain effectively screened out.

Animals abound but with less shrieking bedlam than on the other side of the plateau. Many of them leap and swing toward us, primates, mostly larger variations of Earth's chimpanzee, gibbon, orangutan, gorillas. And of course whoofies.

"Joss," Emerald gasps, gripping my hand.

The animals have quickly massed and are suddenly a screeching, screaming hoard racing pell-mell toward all of us.

I reach for Emerald to shelter her in my arms, but in this terrifying stampede I have only the armor of my fragile body. If we fall, we will be crushed.

We are overrun—and bypassed, the animals rushing to open-armed women all around us, to be welcomed with fervor. Openmouthed, I watch women tumble over the ground in their greeting of these animals as if they are all much-loved friends, a display of kinship with the animal kingdom that Emerald and I witness in awe.

An hour later, our wonderment and fascination continue undiminished: The women and animals frolic like children at playtime. It is compelling, moving, and I watch with envy, admiration, and an infinite loneliness.

A few of the women and the gorillas have gone running off into the jungle. They reappear bearing armfuls of fruit and leaves filled with what turns out to be apricot-size nuts.

Several of the women deposit offerings nearby, and assuming this is their intent, we help ourselves. I'm more thirsty than hungry, but I taste what everyone around us is consuming—varied fruit reminiscent of banana, avocado, apple, and citrus; the citrus is of such high-juice content that it quickly slakes my thirst. The nuts taste of pistachio subtly infused with soy. The food is delicious, satisfying.

Many of the animals are melting away into the jungle, as if by signal. The women and children around us, and the animals that remain—dozens all told—mill around in the gloom of the jungle and carefully choose only the clearest patches of ground away from trees. Almost in unison, they sink to the ground about a meter equidistant from one another. They stretch out prone, legs outspread, arms raised; and rub their faces into bare soil in a manner that seems blissful, some licking soil from their lips. Each one, as she achieves whatever satisfaction she seeks, lies perfectly still and closes her eyes.

"What in the world..." Emerald breathes. She grips my arm as if she seeks more solid assurance of my presence.

I can only shake my head.

We sit motionless, watching. Amid all the activity in the trees around us, a palpable calmness and harmony have descended. Except for the rise and fall of their breathing, none of the bodies move; even their respiration seems to be slowing with each passing moment, until it too becomes scarcely perceptible. The beautiful nude bodies, of every skin tone, arms raised in what seems exaltation, look like fallen classic statuary.

Some long minutes later, when the scene has changed not a whit, Emerald leans into me and says quietly, as if she might awaken the motionless bodies, "What should we do?"

I get to my feet and help her to hers. I lead us away a short distance, into an area of the jungle with more abundant ground cover, where we can sit amid ankle-high vines and talk comfortably while we watch our prone, immobile companions.

"Maybe it's a kind of sleep," she offers.

I nod. "If it is, it seems a very deep sleep, like a coma."

"They're not afraid of anything, Joss."

"No. They're not." I envy them.

Emerald sits contemplating them, knees drawn up, elbows on her knees, chin cupped in her hands. "This is what seems to make sense so far. The plateau where we were: They go up there when the rain stops. Eat, make love through the night. They come down here in the day hours, out of the rain, play with all their animal friends, and sleep during the day. What do you think?"

I can attest to the nighttime lovemaking part of it. "It's a good hypothesis. It may be a kind of mass meditation, though," I say, gesturing to them. "A trancelike state."

"Maybe. We don't know enough yet."

All I know is that the newest generations have regressed. They've sunk into this primitive existence...I don't want to exchange more theories. I only want to appreciate the sublime bodies laid out before us and let my mind wander back to the events of the night. Whatever my disadvantages in the sexual realm, each woman did enjoy me and enjoyed me fully, more than once. My memory of their raptures grows more and more intimate...

I sense, feel eyes on me, and turn. The wordless intent in her gaze is unmistakable.

"From the start I was drawn to you," Emerald says.

"And I to you," I confess, "from the moment we met."

"I don't know what will happen to us," she says. "I only know what I want right now."

Her body is so sweet, so tender, so supple and soft in my hands that as I caress her, I wish I could be in other bodies simultaneously to bring her the pleasures that were given to me. Her hands cup my face, and she brings my lips to hers, and I discover with an accompanying inundation of pleasure something I did not experience last night: intimacy. No one kissed my lips; my tongue was never touched by another's like this; no one's arms wound tenderly around my neck and shoulders; no one's body met mine with such shy yearning.

Kissing her, my tongue in slow caress of hers, I lower her into the ferns, wanting only to love her with all the gentleness in me, all the generosity my arms and body and lips can summon for her. Yet, as I caress her, I feel a bold sureness building within me: I cannot be all the women of the night, but I can be each of them at a time and bring to her all those pleasures they so confidently brought to me.

A timeless while later, as Emerald moans from my fingers moving assertively within her, I taste her, but all too briefly: at the first stroking of my tongue she convulses around my fingers. And so, sometime afterward, when the quivering of her thighs, the tension of her body, tell me she is open to me again, I again bathe my lips in the wetness of her, and it is not my fingers but my tongue that enters her for a long unhurried while as her hips undulate fiercely in my hands, and I savor the woman-taste and woman-scent that I love...again and again.

Afterward, if she is surprised by my fulsome ardor and that I require nothing in return, she does not speak it. "I knew you would be the most wonderful lover," she murmurs in exhaustion and collapses into sleep in my arms. I sense we are being observed—perhaps by animals, since the women have not moved. But I don't care. I too drowse in the heat and peace of the day.

I am awakened not by any particular sound but by a feeling that I need to be conscious. I have no idea how much time has passed; the gloom of where we lie entwined seems unchanged. But all around me the women, their strange ritual over, are preparing to move off.

I kiss Emerald awake and lift her to her feet. With my arm

around her, she moves sleepily against me, in step with me as we follow the women.

As Emerald had forecast, we retrace our steps to our plateau. Where the rain continues, but under diminishing clouds. Again I join the women in raising my arms to the cleansing downpour.

The day ending, the rain ending, we drink our fill of the nectar-like water at the pool, and then turn our attention to renewed mounds of fresh flowers. When and by whom this food is provided and where it originates remains a mystery, but an underlying rationale to the universe of these women is emerging, and after three days here I sense a rhythm and order, albeit unique.

Emerald and I gather a bouquet of the flowers, each of us searching for favorites of the night before, and settle ourselves to eat and drink. I quickly consume the first flower and all of its contents—honey, berry, and nutmeg flavors—eager to know if I will again experience that same euphoric opening of my senses as the night before.

I do. With every sip of the flowery brew, the very molecules within me seem to open out to the spectacular star-flung firmament, my body basking in the tropical evening air bathed with those scents that, like last night, seem intoxicants by themselves. I can only wonder what else may be duplicated this night, whether the women will reappear, the three for Emerald, and the three for me…

Three women do approach. I have not seen them before, but like last night, one of them extends a hand to Emerald. This time she refuses it, saying to me, "They're not doing this again. I'm staying here with you."

Over her shoulder I see other women assemble in the shadows. "You should go," I tell her firmly.

"*Go?*" She looks at me incredulously. "I don't understand you. It was 'don't go' last night—you *insisted*. But tonight—*tonight…*" Her face is stiff with hurt and anger.

"Emerald, listen to me. You were right last night when you said we don't know what they want. We need to find out. We can't stay here. Both of us need to follow any direction we're given to get ourselves out of here." It is the truth, if not the entire truth.

A withering glance tells me her opinion of my opinion. She thrusts her hand into the hand of the woman, yanks herself up, and marches off. I see in her lengthening footsteps her fury that I am sending her off after what has happened between us this day.

I have a higher priority, I tell myself.

But with her disappearance into the gloom I cannot ignore or deny the increase in my heartbeat as those from the shadows approach. None are from last night, and they number five. Aspects of the five are the same: They are of varied and beguiling beauty; and they too have removed their breast bands. Their intention appears to be the same as last night, and I feel a quailing that there are five, when last night three were quite enough—more than enough.

Whatever they intend to do with me, it will not begin here. Two of them extend a hand, pull me to my feet, and place me between them, continuing to clasp my hands as we head into forest cloaked in deep shadows.

A brief time later we come out into a clearing, and they stop, release my hands, and surround me. For a breathless time they stand motionless. I look down, completely unnerved. The woman directly in front of me reaches for my hand, and I look up at her into her coral eyes. Illuminated in moonlight, as if in a spotlight, is the gleaming pale perfection of her form. She releases my hand to turn herself in slow rotation. One after another, they take my hand and turn for me, and I am allowed to gaze in full at their naked beauty, alabaster to ebony, slender and supple to richly fleshed.

Two of the women bring my hands to their breasts: Smooth firm globes overflow my palms and fingers; other hands, from behind me, cup and then caress my breasts, other hands clasp, slide down over my thighs. A pervasive humming has begun.

I will not be a passive recipient this night. I lean toward the breast in my hand and savor the nipple, berry-sweet and gratifyingly stiffening in my mouth.

I am backed into a mound. Slowly lowered. Onto a kind of platform of leaves, slightly raised, no larger than my body, yielding but firm under my weight. Four women kneel, two on either side of me, and bend over me, down to me. Even in this balmy night the breath that bathes my ears sends shivers through me.

Two women fondle each breast, their palms and fingers imparting separate pleasures; and when they lower their faces to my breasts, I close my eyes and shudder with those sensations—and from the hands exploring my body, moving slowly down my stomach, sliding up inside my thighs, and under me, fingertips moving into the crevasse between my hips in a bold intimacy that expels the breath from my body.

Humming inhabits me. As tongues softly trace my ears, each nipple is gently or roughly sucked and stroked. Sets of fingernails graze my stomach, my thighs, between my legs.

The hum intensifies and with it my sensations, agonies of pleasure. For an eternity I arch again and again in a frenzy of need for what they so endlessly postpone. Then, at last, my contorting thighs are fully spread, and I arch for a final blessed time under the laving of an exquisitely vibrating tongue...

The message this time does not come at the height of rapture but at its convulsing beginning, when I can least comprehend it. But it registers somewhere, and as my body begins to settle in the blissful aftermath of release, it emerges:

SHE WILL DESTROY
ALL OF YOU

In the stark sobering clarity of this message, I ask aloud, "What do you mean? Who is 'she'? Who is 'all of you'?" The questions are futile—these women have not spoken and do not speak now—and I subside into thought. *How will the destruction be done? And most critically,* why? *Why and when will this happen?*

Something else is clear. The events of last night showed me to be, in the fourth try, a viable if limited receptor. The message tonight arrived sooner, in the first try, and this is the first message of the night: As I lie here with my heart rate slowly decelerating, the women surrounding me show no indication of departing. Other messages—perhaps answers—will be delivered throughout this night as I am made ready by these five to receive them.

It is intimidating in the extreme that more than three have come to me tonight to—in the truest sense of the term—consummate this process. And that my naked body is laid out for their every intention on a platform disquietingly symbolic of an altar.

Why me and not Emerald? I wonder, when she is of this planet, an ancestor of theirs, and I am not. Perhaps it's for that exact reason: because I am not of this planet.

Rational thought is flung asunder: satiny, luxuriant breasts are being lowered, melded into mine, swelling thighs embrace mine. I slide my arms around this woman who is the most lavishly fleshed of them and greedily accept the magnificently voluptuous body given to me, tasting her shoulders, my hands clasping and exploring the ample curves of her hips. When she moves her body upward, I eagerly take what is offered, the rich heaviness of her breast in my mouth.

Their intent matches mine: I am meant to participate tonight, a meaning made even clearer when the woman pulls herself up to kneel astride me, cradling my face between her thighs. I part her lips with my tongue and pull her down to me and discover in full measure what I felt between my legs last night, a berry-size protuberance. Its fragrance is of beginning rain, its taste an amalgam of salt and cinnamon and copper, and it vibrates against my tongue, its taste becoming richer with its every vibration. The woman above me rocks in abandon with each stroke of my tongue, her breasts swinging.

Fingers, vibrating fingers, have entered me. I am giving pleasures and awash with my own and am rapidly rising toward orgasm when the woman eases herself away from my tongue and the fingers leave me. She moves quickly back down my bereft body and between my legs, lifts my hips onto her thighs, spreads my legs, and fits her vibrating self within, reigniting me as if she had never left, rocking fiercely, insistently into me. Orgasm is so fiery in its mutuality that in its deliciously lingering aftermath—she continues to oscillate, her face suffused with pleasure—I at first think I have been given no message because of its very intensity, that the stars and nebulae I saw were part of the heights to which I've been taken.

Then I understand that I was meant to receive this image. And that a new experience, another type of message has begun.

My body, so limited in comparison with theirs, is a novelty to these women and perhaps one they mean to fully explore. Perhaps what is happening tonight is so different in its intimacy from last night because my heartfelt loving of Emerald was indeed being observed today.

The one who has just taken me kneels beside me and cradles my face so tenderly in her hands that I no longer care about motives or thought of any kind, only that she is kissing me, and with deep, unhurried, strokes of her sensitive tongue. And sometime later her stroking in me is an intense counterpoint to another tongue vibrating within me.

I am turned onto my stomach by one of them, and the vibrating tongue in the cleft between my hips accompanied by the vibrating fingers between my legs brings me such new intensities of ecstasy and visions, that afterward I am reluctant to be turned again onto my back.

Until the next woman settles her smooth thighs between my face and I am offered her almond-earthy tastes to savor. I have lost all track of any awareness except being subsumed into the passion of the women taking me in different inventions until I can no longer distinguish between the fusion of sensation and the visions that accompany them.

I taste each woman in every measure. I writhe in exquisite pleasure under a vibrant tongue that does not stroke but endlessly flicks.

Once more, after the fully fleshed woman once again fiercely rocks between my thighs, words, not visions, come to me:

TO KNOW

There is to be more, and I am turned over on my stomach to have that extraordinarily intense pleasure visited on me again, in a finale that renders me exhausted and capable only of understanding the final message of the night:

TO KNOW
YOU MUST STAY

PERSONAL JOURNAL OF OLYMPIA

At the landing site the rain falls unabated, and our party scatters to shelter as best it can within our various ships. Because of its communication capabilities, Megan and Danya will set up the *Sarah Bernhardt* as command headquarters; our flitters' systems are useful only within a very limited continental range. These tiny craft have performed valiantly, considering they were never intended for the use to which we have put them, to venture anywhere beyond Femina.

Minerva and I climb into our flitter and stand in dismay. It may be my overactive imagination, but despite Danya's assurances that our flitter is firmly anchored, it seems to teeter on its perch, threatening to plunge us into the Vanessa River. This thin-skinned craft in such a rain is like having a contingent of manic drummers beside our eardrums. Minerva takes my hand and leads us back out into the rain.

"You are Minerva the historian," I shout over the downpour. "You need to be with Megan."

"Of course I do," she shouts back. "Let the younger ones enjoy the percussion."

We take up residence in the *Sarah Bernhardt* without opposition, perhaps because we are of the Inner Circle and age has its privileges, more likely because it's evident we will brook no opposition. Soon we are joined by Venus and Vesta. And thereafter by other members of our party until the *Sarah Bernhardt* is crowded with all twenty of us.

Minerva and I, being first onboard, are in the less crowded command module with Megan and Danya. Megan is the personification of distress, Danya the picture of frustration. No more so than I. An optimum team cannot be assigned to the search for Hera, Tara, and my Ceeley because all of them are here on Amazonia, having joined the search for Emerald and Joss.

"We're doing everything you would do," Mother has assured us.

Erika adds in confirmation, "We've concentrated six drones in the vicinity of Gearhart Island, but unfortunately the progress of the typhoon has slowed—to a land speed of only five kilometers per hour. Weather in that sector is expected to clear sometime tomorrow morning. We'll have the *Natalie Barney* in the air and will land the moment we can."

What is significant is what they have not told us: that they have picked up any readings from Gearhart Island. A ship must indeed be dispatched to that sector, but I know in the most dismal depths of my soul that its mission may be to recover bodies.

"It's perhaps of no consolation," Danya tells Megan, "but this is what we experienced when you and Minerva left to return to Earth and we had no further word from you."

"You are correct, Danya," Megan replies icily. "It is of no consolation."

The day that passes is perhaps the slowest and most agonizing of my life. Messages are coming in from the loved ones of all the missing. Megan is in communication with Laurel, each of them trying to buoy the other with hope that their daughter will be found.

We can go nowhere. We can do nothing but watch the negative reports coming in, watch the rain that becomes more funereal with every passing hour.

Finally—the first good thing to happen. With sundown has come the cessation of the rain, the rapid parting and dissolution of the clouds, and the emergence of something approaching normalcy—our royal-blue night and the splendor of our skies.

We come out of our ships into humid tropical air that instantly makes me want to discard my robe even though my body temperature is well regulated within its confines. The supplies on the various ships will form our communal meal, and it augurs to be a most delicious one since Vesta has taken control and is already combining ingredients with her usual alchemy.

On Megan's order, two flitters lift off, taking advantage of the clear weather for surveillance of the immediate area. With ill-equipped craft, and pilots able to use only hand-held sensors, I hold little hope that we will have any sightings from the air. We don't.

After a repast over which others exclaim but I scarcely taste, Megan gives an order in her clear bell tones: "Bring out every light bar we have."

She does not have to explain the reason. What needs explaining is why no one else thought of creating our own, very basic signal beacon.

Women come from every craft carrying every implement that sheds light. We build them into a gigantic pyramid that illuminates every inch of our site and radiates its glow high into the dark sky. We sit around it like shipwrecked sailors at a campfire, talking softly, staring into the gloom as if we are the ones awaiting rescue.

We started out with two missing, and our efforts have resulted instead in five missing—an outcome no one would have dreamed except in nightmare. None of us has voiced our truest fear: that Hera, Tara, and Ceeley have been lost at sea; and that Emerald and Joss, with their E-bands inoperative, have been attacked, dragged into the depths of the jungle—and if we somehow are able to locate them, what we will find will be bones.

It is now very late this night. Most of the women are arranging themselves to sleep out under our moons and stars; some are already asleep. Minerva and I will return to the *Sarah Bernhardt* to spend the night in comfort more befitting our years. And to hope that another day will bring a better result.

Never has anything seemed more futile to me. Never have I felt so desolate. So isolated and so lonely.

PERSONAL JOURNAL OF JOSS

I brace myself for Emerald's return. For the unhappiness and anger she will surely direct toward me, either with caustic words or punishing silence.

My behavior would be inexplicable to anyone. Three days ago I could only dream that some day Emerald's love might be attainable. I would not have imagined spending an afternoon of passion with so beautiful a woman, that this could ever be in the realm of the possible. That it indeed happened, and I then allowed her to be taken away from me the same night for what could only seem to her the most specious of reasons, will have a predictable result. I see her now in the distance over the top of a wave.

"Joss!" She runs toward me, her slender nude body lovely in the morning light. Arms up, waving her hands, calling "Joss! Joss!"

What's happened? I run to meet her.

"Joss! Did you see it?"

"See what?"

"The light last night!"

I shake my head, and she puts her hands on her hips and looks at me as if my intelligence has surely leaked out of my brain. "How could you not see it? It lit up the entire sky to the west of us. Where the *Sarah Bernhardt* is! They've come for us!"

Elated, I dash up a wave to look to where she points. Then, sheepishly, I walk back to her, embarrassed by my notion that I might actually see them.

So a rescue party arrived yesterday, somehow managed to land on that outcropping beside the Vanessa River, and signaled their presence last night by lighting up the night sky. While I was otherwise fully occupied. Undoubtedly, had I seen any irregular light last night, I would have ascribed it to the pyrotechnics of orgasm.

"Fortunately, one of us managed to be awake," she says scathingly. "Apparently you can sleep through anything."

I do not reply. Today I have even more reasons not to reveal what was done to me last night.

"We need to get out of here, Joss. I tried to find you last night as soon as I saw the signal—where were you?"

"They took me in there." I gesture vaguely at a more thickly wooded area of our plateau.

"What for?"

I parry, "Why did they take you where they took you?"

She shakes her head, waving a hand in irritation. "We need to get out of here," she repeats. "We need to get our clothes and—whoever's come for us, they'll never find us in here. How long will they wait? We have to go. We know the general direction. This is our one and only chance."

It has begun to rain hard. Hands on her hips, Emerald looks around at the women who are beginning their day just as they did yesterday, standing with arms raised to its restorative powers. "Let's do this, Joss. Let them try and stop us."

I wonder if they will, but for very different reasons than Emerald's. I wonder if they will let her go but stop me.

We find and don our clothes and set off. The women make no attempt to stop us. Clearly, it will be up to me to determine what I will do from here with the messages I've received.

They follow us. A group of perhaps twenty, keeping pace with Emerald's quick strides across the pyramid, and down its side and through the terrain that leads to the thickest part of the jungle.

Whether she is simply intent on her journey, or has renewed her anger, Emerald does not look at me or speak to me.

As we arrive where we must enter the wiry tangle of jungle, the women all move in front of us.

"They mean to lead," I suggest.

"Yes, but to where?" she says suspiciously. "Can we trust that they intend to bring us back?"

"No more than we can trust anything else they do. But I think we need to take that chance. We'll lose all orientation once we get into the jungle."

She nods, and I reach out to her, saying, "It's best we don't get separated."

Swallowing whatever reluctance she may feel about my touch, she surrenders a hand to me. And we go in together, and the jungle swallows us, and seems more impassable than before—blinding, smothering, choking, constraining.

An unknowable misery of an exhausting time later, we come stumbling out and collapse into the clearing where Emerald had found her daughter, where she had concealed the chain. Except for traversing the channel to the Vanessa River, we're back.

"Why?" Emerald says in exasperation, and extracts her hand from mine. Brushing pollens from her clothes, turning her face up to the lightly falling rain for its cleansing properties, she asks, "Why in the world did they take us where they did? Why did they do this—this whole exercise?"

"That's the question that needs to be answered," I offer, and she tosses me a glance that conveys disgust at my seemingly simplistic answer.

"Let's go," she says abruptly, then runs into the channel.

I now know what I will do: I follow her. And the women follow me.

PERSONAL JOURNAL OF MINERVA

It is midmorning on this second day after our landing on Amazonia, the third since we left Femina in search of Joss and Emerald.

The night was one of the longest of my life, as undoubtedly it was for us all. With hope fading that we will find any of our missing five alive, I continued to berate myself for every cross word spoken between my sister Hera and me, to vow that henceforth, if she should be restored to us, I would forevermore forego any challenge to her arrogance. I know that my sister Olympia, in despair over both Hera and Ceeley, managed only a few minutes' light doze at best. Pale and drawn, she has refused food and sips only tea, as does Megan, and we all quietly await the next step, the reports from the *Natalie Barney;* it will shortly land on Gearhart Island. We will then hold a strategy meeting to gather input from all of us who have ventured here to Amazonia. Beginning with dawn, the heavy rain has resumed, adding to the somberness of mood.

I expect no positive news from Gearhart Island, and I see only two alternatives for our own landing party, both of them bleak. One is to remain for a finite time while we take the limited action open to us to locate Emerald and Joss. The other is to abandon what seems, in hindsight, to be an ill-conceived and disastrous rescue attempt and to limp home on the *Sarah Bernhardt* and our other craft to begin the healing of very deep wounds.

If I were Megan and it were my daughter out there, I would simply order the former option: to stay and wait and search wherever we can until hope dies. None of us would question the order; she is our leader. But as our leader she has made some very difficult, personally costly choices that are part of our history, and I know she will do so now—perhaps none so difficult as this one, though, nor with such personal consequence… If we abandon the search for Emerald, Megan must return to Femina and face Laurel with the consensus she has accepted about their daughter's fate.

It is now an hour later. With all of us packed into the confines of the *Sarah Bernhardt*, Megan convenes our meeting, standing before us straight and slender, arms crossed, the sleeves of her white shirt rolled up to the elbows.

"Word has come in from Gearhart Island," she says without preamble. I cannot imagine how she can maintain the evenness of her tone. I am well aware of the grim news she will deliver, and anyone who so much as glances at Danya's face, or that of Olympia and myself, will know the nature of that news. We are shaken; we clutch each other's hands for support. Vesta sits with us but is herself distressed and in any case can offer little from her healing arts to assuage the brunt of what we confront.

"The *Eleanor Roosevelt* and *Marie Curie* are intact, having held their moorings through the force of the storm," Megan announces. "The *Margaret Mead* remains partially moored, and the destruction to her is considerable."

The visuals draw gasps from everyone assembled: The *Mead* lies flipped over on her back and ripped open; pieces of her float on the sunlit coral waters of the ocean.

Megan says, "We found no traces of our sisters anywhere on the island—"

Another gasp, a rising murmur that quickly subsides as Megan continues, "—but flitters from the *Barney* are patrolling the ocean waters, and our drones continue in search pattern."

I feel only despair. If their flitter did manage to escape the *Mead,* what would the odds be for survival in the kind of ocean turbulence created by a monster typhoon?

"We must now consider our options—"

Megan is interrupted by a sudden, most considerable commotion at the rear of the group, near the entry to our ship.

"Mother!"

Emerald. It is Emerald, pushing her way through the throng of us toward Megan. And behind her, Joss, making her way toward Olympia and me.

Amid the bedlam, as I clasp Joss to me in an embrace that threatens to crush her ribs, I feel a powerful, renewing surge of optimism. If the safe return of these two is possible, then—no matter what the odds—why not continue to hold out hope for Hera, Tara, and Ceeley?

Joss has stepped aside and allows Emerald, standing with her mother's arm around her shoulders, to relate their adventures, and we all take in the amazing and puzzling events of what has transpired the last few days: their landing, how they returned to find the *Sarah Bernhardt* with vital equipment missing, then were shunted off by a contingent of young women to a strange, leaf-covered pyramid where they have spent the last days and nights.

Emerald is so happy, and the rest of us are so elated, that no one is willing at this moment to reveal the dismal news about our missing sisters. Joss, however, seems distant and unusually subdued, given the circumstances of her return to us. It would not surprise me if she has sensed something amiss.

"We found the *Bernhardt* in perfect working order except for the beacon," Danya informs Emerald and Joss.

Emerald just shakes her head as if this is simply one more inexplicable act. "They must have restored everything after they took us with them."

The women who accompanied Joss and Emerald back to us are visible through the *Bernhardt*'s windows. "They've returned you here—why do they remain?" I ask. They stand or sit in the rain, indifferent to it, in casual nudity and perfect comfort, as if patiently waiting—for what, I cannot imagine.

"I assure you," Emerald says acerbically, "there's no rationale for anything they do or don't do."

Joss says quietly, "They wait for me."

Only silence greets this astounding statement. Emerald gapes at her.

"I need to return with them," Joss adds.

"*Why?*" The word is an expulsion from Emerald. "What's *happened* to you? Joss—"

"I can tell you now: They're giving me information."

"*What* information?"

"It's still coming together. That's why I need to go back."

"You're telling me this only *now*? Why didn't you—"

"It was our circumstances. I couldn't."

"What, why—" Emerald sputters, her face choleric with anger.

"What kind of information?" Megan asks Joss, tightening her arm around the shoulders of her distraught daughter.

"It's urgent, Megan, having to do with the future of our Unity. I've been chosen to receive it, and it's critically important that I stay here."

"Joss," Olympia says softly from beside me, "there's something you need to know. Tara is missing."

Joss stands perfectly still as Olympia summarizes the events of the last few days—our attempt to mount a rescue mission, our encounter with the typhoon, the disastrous consequences.

Vesta has been quietly watching Joss. Joss, head bowed,

rubs her face with her hands. What more, I wonder, could possibly happen in her young life?

Lifting her head, looking around at us all, Joss says, "I have to entrust the search for her to you—I have no other choice."

Emerald looks pleadingly at Vesta. "She's delusional. We ate strange food while we were with them. It's affected her, it must have. Please—you must make her stay."

If Joss has been affected by something she ingested, why wouldn't it have the same effect on Emerald? Still, there is an element of truth in what she contends—from the moment Joss arrived, she has seemed present in body only, her focus somewhere beyond us. But each member of our Unity, unless she performs an act that inflicts harm on another, is accorded total personal freedom. Joss choosing to remain here, however much pain and hurt it may bring, cannot be construed as harm. Vesta can offer what psychological input she deems appropriate but cannot violate the terms of our charter. We cannot prevent Joss from returning with these women to a mysterious world inaccessible to the rest of us, if that is what she chooses to do.

In truth, as a historian I agree with the necessity, if not the urgency, of gleaning insights into this most baffling of generations, and if Joss can unlock anything to explain what has happened to cause so complete an alienation, it would be an enormous service to us.

Vesta reaches to Joss, takes her hands. Searching her face, she asks softly, "Joss, these women do not speak. How are they imparting this information to you?"

Joss hesitates, then says, very carefully it seems to me, "It's a kind of mind-meld."

"What kind—"

"I wish to say no more, esteemed Vesta."

"Joss, this is your irrevocable decision?"

"It is."

Vesta nods. "We accept your decision."

I look to Emerald for the protest I expect. "As do I," she says unexpectedly. "I trust you. I have to trust what you say. Just come back to...just come back to us."

Emerald is in love with her. I can see it. We all can.

Megan says, "We have no means of communication with you, but we'll leave a flitter secured here for your return."

"Thank you, Megan," Joss says. "I'll indeed return the moment I gain what I need. Esteemed Vesta, may I have a private word with you and Minerva?"

There is only one place we can go for privacy. But before I can lead the way, our sisters move as one, and they themselves depart the *Bernhardt* into the downpour and accord us isolation.

As soon as we're alone, Joss says to us, "I need to ask an enormous favor of you both."

"Of course, Joss," I tell her. Vesta nods and smiles.

Joss detaches the tiny seed of the recorder pendant from her throat, removes the chain securing it around her neck, and hands them both to me. "I have submitted the entry code," she says.

I am frozen in place, scarcely believing my eyes and ears. Vesta is similarly shocked. Perhaps Joss is indeed mentally impaired.

Joss reaches to me, takes my limp hand, places the recorder in my palm, closes my fingers around it. "You need to know what's happened to me since I've been here. In case Emerald's correct—that I'm delusional. Both of you need to assess what's here, in confidence, until I return."

I stare into my palm. Not many of us choose to use a personal recorder, the most intimate diary possible of our lives. Few of us can manage to be entirely comfortable with a device that holds our innermost thoughts, feelings, reactions, no matter how safeguarded it may be with an identity code. Those of us who use a recorder often share individual perceptions of important events, but this always, always involves editing out that which we deem private—all of us understand that. Not one of us would surrender our recorder fully to another. Not one of us, to my knowledge, ever has. No one I've known has had the courage to unlock and expose so final a bastion of personal privacy. It is as if she surrenders to us her soul.

Joss says quietly, "I believe our Unity is in great peril. It's my duty to find out how and why. When I return, time may be of the essence."

I nod. I trust Joss implicitly.

"Minerva, the trust I require from you is ultimate. In return for my recorder I need another. I need it for what will happen to me now."

Without hesitation I place a fingertip on my recorder, mentally recite my entry code and authenticate it with the required nine variations, remove the recorder, place it in her palm, and close her fingers around it.

"Esteemed Minerva, I promise that only what happens from this moment forward—I promise I will never access—"

"Joss, I know. What I *don't* know is why you are again the one to carry enormous burdens for us."

"Perhaps," Vesta says, "it's simply because she is able to. Be careful, Joss."

I clasp her shoulders, feeling the substance of them as I look into her face, into her calm gray-blue eyes and the determination in them. "Go with my love," I tell her.

"With the love and gratitude of us all," Vesta adds.

Joss nods and backs away, staring at us as if she is memorizing our faces. She leaves the ship. I watch from the windows as the young women of this continent of Amazonia immediately take up position around her. Moments later they all vanish in the rain.

PERSONAL JOURNAL OF OLYMPIA

It goes without saying that Vesta will reveal nothing of what she has gleaned from her contact with Joss. And I respect that Minerva also will not divulge anything of what Joss has said to her in confidence, nor even hint at the topic of Joss's private meeting with these two.

But I feel anger. And yes, jealousy. Joss is more than just my protégé—I have taken her into my affections over these recent years and hold her close to my heart. I feel a most personal betrayal, and it combines with the bitter betrayal I feel toward every aspect of this world. I came here for its promise, to spend the concluding years of my life with my sisters in an idyllic society. I have found only grief and pain, isolation, estrangement. And now, because of our presence here, because Joss accompanied Emerald on a quixotic journey to a place where neither should have ventured, they have set in motion events that have cost me the woman I love most—

"A flitter!"

I don't know who shouts this; I simply glance out the window of the *Bernhardt*. And see nothing.

"A flitter!"

Another voice, but this time I can identify the speaker. Zera, one of the members of Danya's security team assigned surveillance duties to safeguard our craft from any unexpected event.

A jumble of voices:

"Down the river—"

"Zoomed past—"

"Picked it up on—"

"*Saw* it with—"

"Danya!" Megan shouts over all the voices. "Get our flitters in the air!"

Minerva grabs me and screams "It's them!" directly into my ear.

My head ringing, I do not believe what seems to be happening. Our six flitters lurch from their harbor against the *Sarah Bernhardt,* lift into the air, and fly into formation behind us toward the jungle.

"*There!*" screams Minerva again, pointing.

A flitter is dimly visible over the Vanessa River, coming quickly into focus as it careens precipitously toward us, oscillating wildly in the rain. Its air jets hit our rock, it bounces forward, skitters toward us.

Tara. I see Tara at the controls.

"*Brace!*" shouts Megan.

There is no time. It crashes into us, and the *Sarah Bernhardt* bucks from the impact, throwing me off my feet.

No matter. I am on my feet again, and we are all out in the rain, running, running, and for the first time I am grateful for the pouring rain—there will be no fire from the impact.

Megan and three others pull them out of their safety restraints, as if their craft is indeed on fire, while all around us our six flitters return to their moorings. The rest of us help carry Tara, Hera, and yes, my Ceeley, into the *Sarah Bernhardt.*

I will need to consult my recorder for the particulars of all that has transpired over the past two hours. And I will do so;

I intend to commit to memory every blessed detail of what now seems a blur.

For the present moment, I know that the medikits on board have sufficed to treat all the injuries, that we are fortunate neither neurological damage nor internal injuries are involved. Hera's broken leg and collarbone, tended to by Demeter, are close to being fully fused. Both of Tara's broken arms and her skull fracture have fused and her lacerations are bonded. And Ceeley came through the ordeal of their flight and the crash landing with a minor concussion and deep, full-body bruising that has already disappeared with sonic treatment. I know the bruises are gone because I have held her in my arms these entire two hours while she drifted in and out of sleep, and she has expressed no discomfort, only contentment.

I did ask her: "How many more times do I need to almost lose you?"

"Never again," was her whispered reply.

And that is why I have lain beside her and held her all this while, because she is mine to hold. My lips touch her face and hair as she sleeps—a sweetly lined face of softest texture after all the years, her once autumn-brown hair lightened by gray—and I inhale the scents of her, and with every breath, with every passing moment, my parched soul is renewed.

All three survivors—oh, so wonderful a word—lie on inflata-cots in the main cabin of the *Bernhardt*. Now that their injuries have been treated, Tara is deeply asleep as a necessary part of her final healing, but Hera, the intelligence in her dark eyes glazed from transfusions of plasma, nutrients, restoratives, and sedative, her body swaddled in a blanket further infused with nostrums, has refused this step until she speaks of what happened, knowing all of us burn to know.

With Megan, Minerva, and Demeter seated beside her, Hera begins in a whispery voice: "I had one mooring rod in and was securing the other. A gust lifted one edge of the *Mead* and turned us ten degrees—"

"That would be enough," Danya mutters.

"Yes, Danya—the weight distribution." Hera's voice is firming as she speaks. "The next gust put us broadside, and then *Mead*'s lighter aft was pulled around, and we had our flitter facing into the wind instead of away from it. We couldn't power her out—she was too light for winds like those. We were trapped, we had no options. If I cut the *Mead* loose, we'd have been blown backward into the ocean. With higher winds coming in and only one mooring, I knew we'd get battered. And we were. The flitter was safest place we could be. But even inside it, even in restraints..." She closes her eyes briefly against the memory. "Then the *Mead* flipped over. That's when I broke my collarbone, Tara broke an arm, and Ceeley lost consciousness. We were upside-down, but the flitter was still attached to the floor of the *Mead*. But we were being blown apart—"

I listen to this nightmare account with my hand at my throat. I feel grateful Ceeley was not conscious for some of this horror, and that she sleeps again through Hera's recital.

"A tree hit the *Mead,* ripped open a hole, fully exposed us to the wind, and it broke the flitter free and blew us right out of there and straight toward the water. Tara managed a full power surge and barely lifted us clear."

Hera pauses to sip some water. "Our communications didn't extend to you or Femina. Tara and I decided this was our logical landing point. Anywhere else, we didn't think we could survive before anyone found us, or if there would even be a search—you might have thought we died on the island. When we came within range of here, we still couldn't raise you."

"We'd landed and were out of our flitters," Danya says regretfully. "If I'd only known to leave someone inside—"

"Don't be ridiculous," Hera snaps, and it's heartening to see this vestige of her imperious former self, even through the powerful effect of the medication.

"Can I ask—"

"Yes, Danya, hurry," Demeter tells her.

"How did the other three flitters manage to get out of the *Mead* and not you?"

Hera closes her eyes, briefly. "Because I very stupidly disobeyed Megan's order. I thought I could take more time beyond the ten seconds she allotted for mooring the *Mead.* I didn't want my ship destroyed. Instead I very nearly destroyed the three of us."

Minerva speaks: "You're actually admitting you made a mistake?" She smiles at Hera, and there is gentleness in her tone.

"Yes, Minerva. But it's my first mistake of any consequence."

When Minerva says nothing more, Hera manages a weak grin. "Go ahead, Minerva. Tell me I kept the worst for first."

"I would," Minerva responds seriously, "but I made a vow that if you lived—"

"What a ridiculous vow," Hera retorts.

Minerva chooses, with visible effort, to remain silent.

"Minerva, I didn't fight this hard to survive to have you bore me to death with politeness. I want nothing changed between us. I release you from your silly vow. And I'm ready to sleep now."

"All craft," Megan says, grinning, "let's clean up this rock for Joss, and prepare to depart from Amazonia."

"Sleep well, my dear Hera," says a voice from Femina. And adds, "I knew you girls would manage."

PERSONAL JOURNAL OF MINERVA

Joss's first reappearance was a week ago, a highly consequential, if brief, visit of a mere few minutes' duration with no advance notice. She had been gone a month. She literally turned up on my doorstep. Nude. She shook her head at my invitation to enter and handed to me my personal recorder. And said with formal, cool distance, her face expressionless, "I estimate the Unity will require five days for review and assessment. I will return then."

I recovered my wits enough to ask the essential questions: "Joss, what have you learned? What will happen to us? When?"

She simply pointed to my palm and the tiny pendant recorder that suddenly seemed to weigh down my hand. "Joss," I said, "your family—Silke, Tara, Trella—they are most concerned—"

"I must leave," she told me, and the indifference in her tone and in her face was chilling.

"I'll get you another recorder," I said and fled into my house.

But when I returned, she was gone. And this, beyond all else, was the most discomfiting aspect of her return. I could rationalize, somewhat, her postponement of contact with her birth mother or sister. After all, she had not seen

Silke or Trella for years before her arrival here on Maternas. And as for Tara, it's been clear for some time, at least to me, that Joss's feeling for her would not easily survive a serious challenge. But not taking a recorder, abandoning its use...

Joss considers her profession to be music and she is indisputably gifted in that realm. But her eyewitness accounts of the final days of Theo Zedera's reign on Earth have shown her to be a remarkable historian with a keen eye for the scope, context, and essence of events. Who better to assess her ability than I? Aside from her absorption in history, use of a recorder becomes quickly ingrained—indeed, addictive—for all of us who chronicle our lives against the backdrop of historical events, and it is inconceivable to me that she would leave without replacing the one she surrendered and abruptly terminate this lifelong practice.

Be that as it may. Of course Vesta and I reviewed Joss's extraordinary experiences on Amazonia on the first recorder she had given us. In view of the apocalyptic nature of our findings and in view of our promise to Joss that we would assess what she had given us "in confidence," we debated what next step we should take that would not be a blunder, or worse, would in some inadvertent way obstruct a process leading to meaningful insights into our youngest generation and the nature of the ominous future being foretold for us through Joss. The critical urgency of what was communicated in so unorthodox a method dictated our next step, a step made even more obvious by the extraordinary veneration accorded to Mother on her return by our youngest generations.

"My descendants never cease to amaze me," was her first reaction upon viewing Joss's sexual experiences. Then, gazing out from her house at our peaceful Cybele gleaming under sunlit coral skies as she stroked the whoofie in her lap, she counseled, "Await additional information from

Joss. Assuming, with what they're giving her along with the information, she's willing to leave and tell us more."

"Mother, this is serious," Vesta said softly.

"Of course it's serious," she retorted. "Am I supposed to weep and tear my hair until she returns?"

"The earthquakes..." Vesta did not finish.

I nodded my agreement. Of increasing frequency and intensity all over Femina, they seem even more terrifying in context with the unambiguous threat in the messages given thus far to Joss that there is an inimical and ruthless force at work—against which we may be powerless.

"Girls," Mother said, and just the calmness in her voice, the wisdom in her remarkable green eyes, soothed my agitated spirit. "Look at our situation this way. What can we do about what we know so far? Nothing. If we disseminate this information before Joss returns, what do we accomplish?"

With my beloved Christa and our daughter, Celeste, to consider, with Vesta carrying the wider responsibility of the psychological well-being of our Unity, I offered, "We can be prepared."

"For what? All we'll accomplish is create fear," Mother said.

"We *should* be afraid," Vesta argued. "Time may be of the essence, Mother. We're not children. We can face—"

"Face what, Vesta?" Mother demanded. "When we understand that, we'll understand what we must do. Like adults."

We of course acquiesced to her counsel. And awaited Joss's return like raindrops bouncing on a scalding hot surface.

Immediately following Joss's arrival on my doorstep a week ago, Vesta and I collaborated with Mother in viewing the truly shocking contents of the newest recordings. From there we shared it all with Megan and those members of the Inner Circle selected by Mother.

"Not Hera or Venus," Mother decided. "Hera will be

furious at her exclusion, but what we need now is cogent, collaborative thought—we don't have time to deal with her pronouncements. Venus will be a complete distraction with all her swooning over Joss's orgasms."

She did include Diana, Demeter, and Olympia. Their initial, thunderstruck reactions were predictable. Their next responses were a vindication of Mother: They turned to the practicalities as to how we should proceed.

And Joss, true to her word, returned to us when we most needed her presence, two days before we were ready to share with our entire Sisterhood what she has revealed to us. She spent the entire time with Mother, Megan, and myself. She combined the essence of our findings into a narrative whole and discussed her own role in our revelations.

Now, appearing from seemingly nowhere, Joss has just walked into the Council Chambers, her unself-conscious nudity and unkempt hair a discordant note against the careful tableau we of the Inner Circle present with the ceremonial robes we wear for this gravest of days, and the high-collared, formal white shirt and black pants and boots Megan has donned. Hera and Venus stare in open disapproval; understandably, they continue to be peeved and affronted by their exclusion from our consultations and the reasons leading to this planet-wide gathering.

Joss speaks no greeting, nor do we. Our grim faces are more than sufficient to the occasion. She makes her way to our crystal table as if where she will sit is foreordained—and it has been. The smell of her skin and hair reaches me, so reminiscent of pine needles that I feel an unexpected pang of homesickness for Earth.

Joss bows low to Mother, then takes a place beside her at the head of the table. Megan is on the other side of Mother, with myself, Venus, Olympia, Hera, Diana, and Demeter occupying the remainder of the places. Vesta has chosen to be with her team of psychologists among the women in Cybele, a wise decision in my view. Also in our chambers, although not at the council table, are Silke, Emerald, Tara, Trella, and Danya. All of them stare fixedly at Joss—Tara especially; she blinks repeatedly as if she cannot comprehend what she sees. Joss's mother, Silke, and sister, Trella, look away in despair and resignation; they have all too often seen the alienation of younger generations on this world.

Our entire Sisterhood on Maternas follows these proceedings, our signal tally showing one hundred percent: Every member of our Unity has checked in from wherever she is and is receiving clear visuals of these proceedings. Notification was made yesterday: emergency code ten, which spoke for itself. The last time such a priority was issued, Earthmen had entered our solar system. Some of our sisters who prefer to live in isolated outposts remain in their habitats, but most have assembled in various locales. In other times we would have come from everywhere to be together in Cybele to confront emergency circumstances, but the violence of our recent earthquakes has made it far too dangerous to congregate in so large a group in one place.

Seated, Joss folds her hands on the crystal surface of our table, her gaze moving to each of us in turn. When her eyes meet mine, I feel as if something has been absorbed from me into her with nothing given in return, as if hers is a consuming gaze no longer attached to a personal identity.

What has happened to her has transformed her completely. Into what, I am still unable to gauge.

"Joss." Emerald is the first of us to speak to her. "Joss," she repeats, and Joss, with seeming effort, turns and looks at her.

Whatever Emerald means to say, something in Joss's face silences her.

My profession as historian was a prime factor in our decision as to how we will impart our information to the Unity. For this reason I was chosen to be coordinator. The responsibility, outweighing all others in the entirety of my life, is one that I would rather walk on red coals than accept, but I made no argument because I would not wish this duty upon any other of my sisters—and surely not upon Megan, whose daughter is intricately involved and who has carried her full share of leadership burdens in the history of our Sisterhood.

I open our colloquium to the planet of Maternas: "Sisters, we will begin. We know you will give your undivided attention to what we present to you, and we ask your patience until the presentation is fully complete: We face the most perilous time of our existence on this world. We face the decision we must make as a consequence. Explanations must be fully laid out to you as to how and why this day has come."

Mother, Megan, Vesta, and I have painstakingly fashioned the contents of Joss's recordings on Amazonia into a chronology. On view screens and in holograms all over Maternas, our Unity views Joss and Emerald's first contact with the women of Amazonia at the clearing after, not before, Emerald commemorated her daughter, Esme, by leaving her chain at the base of the tree. The chronology will expose nothing of Emerald; it will expose everything of Joss. Because it must.

Next we see Joss and Emerald discovering the sabotage of the *Sarah Bernhardt* at the Vanessa River, then some of their enforced trek in the company of the young women to the pyramid-plateau with its leafy floor. The flowerlike food eaten by Joss and Emerald that night. The separation of Joss and Emerald.

And then begins what the three women do with Joss, in graphic detail, no sound or visual element omitted. Amid the rapt, indeed stunned, attention being given to a segment very familiar to me, I am able to look around. Emerald and Tara are openmouthed in their shock. Joss sits at ease, watching the holograph of herself as if she were having a conversation with these three, not being taken to ecstasy by them again and again. I feel certain that at this moment it is exactly how she feels. I notice that Venus, her color rising, manages frequent, envious glances at Joss even while she watches.

"Why," Hera asks, "why is this—"

"*Hera,*" Mother says.

Hera lapses into silence but fidgets as she watches, as does Venus, but I know the sensual nature of this particular sister so well that I understand it is for an altogether different reason. During Joss's fourth orgasm, when the first message begins, there is no more fidgeting; everyone watches in motionless silence through the next culminations until the message of the night is given:

ALL OF YOU
MUST LEAVE

A hubbub quickly arises, and as quickly ends when Mother raises her hands for silence.

The next segment begins with the morning rains, then the journey down from the plateau; the women in their extraordinary, prolonged familiarity with the animal world; their spread-eagled bodies prone on the bare soil; and afterward the return to the plateau. We show nothing of Joss's lovemaking with Emerald. Then Emerald again being led away from Joss, and the approach of the five for a renewal of night-long sexual congress. As Joss is lowered to the bed of leaves, as this sequence begins, I hear a soft moan from Venus.

Now that the context and method of communication have been made abundantly clear, more of the myriad sexual acts with Joss need not be depicted, only the messages she receives. But the first sexual connection of this night is significant for what it demonstrates. Her arousal is lengthy, her climax more intense and protracted, and unlike the previous night the message arrives not as climax ebbs but as it begins. Sexual experience elevated to this height has opened her more fully as a receptor, and she remains open: the first message of this second night fuses into her more completely than any previous, as do all that follow. And I now know that this particular message is the most important of any:

SHE WILL DESTROY
ALL OF YOU

The amazement and consternation in the faces all around me are echoed, I'm certain, everywhere on Maternas. No one speaks.

From here on, of the messages invested in Joss, all save one are pure imagery, and we show this one now, the instruction directed solely to her:

TO KNOW
YOU MUST STAY

The next segment is of the women leading Joss and Emerald back to the *Sarah Bernhardt;* the reunion with our rescue party; Joss's choice to remain in the Amazonian jungle with her companions; the surrender of her personal recorder in exchange for mine to explain to us her decision.

Then Joss's return to Femina a month later and turning over to me the recorder that holds the essence of what we must next present to the Sisterhood. But for now we begin with the first imagery Joss received during her night with the five women.

Joss's initial assumption that it was orgasmic hallucination is more than understandable. This image and the dozens of interconnected ones that follow are of cosmic conflagrations, huge fireballs exploding into one another and extinguishing into monstrously ballooning interstellar clouds that fling pinwheels of galaxies off into endless, disparate distances in a spectacle so incomprehensibly vast, so violent, with color complexities so volatile, I am certain of only one thing, and Hera confirms it in an awed whisper:

"The birth of the universe."

In a chaos where balance or harmony are nonexistent, stars blaze in uncontrolled fury, gargantuan worlds formed from exploding matter collide with one another as if they were mere asteroids. Most of the smaller bodies produced are in turn blasted into charred, hollow sterility by the pitiless radioactive lethality of nearby novas.

Gravitational force slowly comes into play, asserting its own destructive consequences: space debris caught in these fields pummel worlds with deadly aim and pulverizing destruction, rendering many into drifting asteroid belts and rogue comets. Some worlds somehow survive intact. Methane cloud–choked worlds, worlds sheathed with debris gathered into rings in their gravitational fields and forming shaky alliances, rotating uncertainly in concert with other bodies around gentler suns until they either stabilize or fall into those suns.

Haphazard semblances of planets find refuge within more and more of these systems. Planets achieving their own rotational axis and configuring into viability.

No one is more fascinated, more excited by what she views than astrophysicist Hera, who rocks back and forth in her chair. "Amazing," she whispers, "it's..."

She trails off as a new phase begins, quick glimpses of planetary evolution on many of these viable worlds, conditions forming to support life—confirmation of knowledge we already possess in far more detail than we see here: nearly fifteen billion years presented as necessary context, delivered as if a condensation from some cosmic memory bank of what had actually occurred.

Next are the nascent, fierce struggles to sustain the amniotic and atmospheric conditions that will produce viable organisms. If Maternas and Earth are among these, they are unrecognizable among the mass of such planets. Yet what also becomes clear is what we have learned from our own limited explorations of our proportionately tiny area of the cosmos: life-bearing planets are an infinitesimal few in comparison to the incalculable number of solar systems and galaxies.

More of what were previous theories become factually evident in this imagery. On all life-supporting planets, species evolve and either survive or become extinct according to universal principles. The images given to Joss show many variations of elemental life emerging from primordial ooze, evolving into a multitude of species, some as elegantly simple as two propulsive limbs joined at the top, some as convoluted and fantastical as multiheaded octopi.

Then come a succession of meteor assaults, shockingly unexpected on such pastoral, life-bearing worlds, dealing swift, merciless destruction. Some of the maimed worlds are Earth-like; some resemble Maternas—many such planets have the same blue and white, or coral and ivory colors. "Earth," utters Hera, pointing to the holograph of one devastating strike in particular by a mountainous meteor on a blue-white planet. "That appears to be the continent of Pangaea during the Permian. This might be the pre-Triassic meteor strike at Bedout High off the north coast of Pangaea…" She breaks off, watching along with the rest of us the deadly black dust clouds that swiftly enshroud the planet. If this is indeed Earth, only five percent of ocean life and thirty percent of land species will survive a collision that occurred 250 million years ago.

Other life-bearing planets, a very few, are depicted as either escaping meteor strikes altogether or suffering only minor consequences. On those, a rich diversity of animal life emerges, but only animal life thus far—no humanoids have evolved. While primates abound, unlike those on Earth, they appear to be an end unto themselves and not the forebears of humanoids.

Some worlds, their atmospheres burned away by the savagery of meteor blitzkriegs, do not recover. I suspect that when we have more time for analysis, we may deduce that among these are planets in this particular solar system and Earth's. Other images show planets aging millions of years, through entire epochs before they reestablish viable life, only to be struck down again by meteors. "It looks like Earth again," declares Hera, pointing at the holograph before her. "The Yucatan Peninsula, the Cretaceous-Triassic period—the meteor that extinguished the dinosaurs..." As clouds again thicken into a lethally smothering blanket, Hera looks as distraught as if what she witnesses were occurring at this very moment.

Glancing at Joss, I can only marvel at her demeanor, her composure and equanimity when the fragile vessels of her body and mind have been made the receptacle for these apocalyptic visions.

"Mother," interjects Venus, "isn't that—"

"Verna III," Mother confirms, gazing wistfully at the pristine green planet. "It might well be. If it is, I had no idea we'd been hit by meteorites in previous epochs."

She couldn't have known. The stark difference between her birth planet and the Earth on which she spent so many eventful years of her life is that Verna III is a primitive world with an agrarian society and an oral tradition of passing down its history. After Earth's space probes led to its discovery late in the 22nd century, Verna III declared itself off limits to further contact. Earth's scientists, finding insufficient material value on the planet to warrant conquering and exploitation, did not bother to learn anything further about its "backward" inhabitants, such as their enjoyment of centuries of longevity—a genetic gift Mother has bequeathed to us—and huffily declared Verna III to be incompatible alien life and forbade further interaction. By then the man who would father the original nine of us had managed to smuggle Mother off Verna III, accomplishing this deed by disguising her in the gear of a fellow crewman who had fallen down a hill resulting in, as Mother termed it, "death by stupidity."

The segment ends.

"If we are to believe what we see," Hera declares with her usual self-assurance to our planet at large, "aside from any reason as to why we are seeing it, it is clear that only animal life exists on any planets not significantly struck by meteorites."

Joss speaks: "What is clear is that rise of humanoid life occurs only in the aftermath of planetary catastrophe."

Eyebrows raised as she contemplates Joss, Hera accords this corollary the barest nod, declaiming, "Planetary catastrophe is known as marasmus—the malignant debilitation of a world by planetesimal impacts. How admirable that the human species could arise from such—"

"It is not admirable," Joss says evenly.

Even though I know to expect this response, nevertheless it chills my blood.

While Hera sputters for a suitable riposte to this unexpected contention, Emerald demands, "Meaning what? What does all this *mean*? What does all this have to do with this 'she' who promises to destroy us?"

Joss does not reply. Nor do any of us who know the answer because it will soon be made plain. For me, from the day Christa came into my life, every action I've taken has always been on her and Celeste's behalf, and so I have come to my own conclusions as to what must be done from here, as have Mother and Megan. All of us hold our counsel.

Next comes imagery that invokes only pain. Visuals of our newest generation looking at us out of their remote, alien, coral-hued eyes as if we scarcely exist. Ceasing at earlier and earlier ages to respond to us, ignoring the distressed adults around them as if they can no longer hear. Putting rocks in their mouths, placing themselves prone on the soil like those we saw in Joss's recordings on Amazonia, sleeping together like litters of kittens. Attempting, and finally succeeding, in removing themselves entirely from our society. Familiar images that have struck agony into the hearts of us all.

I brace myself. What will now be shown will tie all the images together and astound every single person who has not previously seen it. I should know—I well remember my own reaction. Everyone of us who first saw it—Mother, Megan, the Inner Circle—were equally dumbfounded.

The imagery is a direct upper view of four extraterrestrial vehicles descending to the surface of Maternas and landing simultaneously in a field of waving ivory grass. They are easily identifiable: the four EVs that so famously left the *Amelia Earhart* in orbit after the journey that first brought us here from Earth. The aperture of EV-1, which has Mother and Megan on board, opens first, and a much younger Megan steps out onto this new world and helps Mother onto the surface. They are followed by the rest of our deliriously joyful landing party. What we see is our original landing on Maternas.

And it is impossible that we see it.

"A composite," Hera says dismissively. "Of what significance is this artist's rendition?"

"It is real," Joss states.

Sputters of astonishment arise from all around us. That such imagery exists cannot be. Prior to our landing, no human being had ever previously set foot on Maternas; therefore, no one could have been present on the surface of this world to record it. Even had they been, neither human nor animal life would have been under the landing jets of those vessels.

"Impossible," Hera retorts. "What we see is in violation of every law of geophysiology—

I take it upon myself to point out, "Geophysiology is an Earth-systems science."

"Which applies here!"

"Esteemed Hera." Megan speaks. "The imagery has been certified—it is authentic beyond all question. Spectral analysis uncovered no edge-traces of a composite and matched precisely every instrument reading of our positioning, every climatic reading we have for the moment of landing, every specific detail we have on our own recorders. Beyond that, there is no possible way Joss, or any of the young women on Amazonia, would have information that not only matches but extends beyond even our own records of our landing."

"Then how—"

My sister, Olympia the philosopher, speaks. "The imagery transmitted to Joss has originated from the only place it could—the consciousness of the planet itself."

Amid all the head-shaking disbelief, the exclamations of incredulity, Joss speaks: "Olympia is correct."

"Psychosis," mutters Hera, and looks away from Joss to the rest of us. "And as for you, you surely cannot believe this—"

"We do believe it," I say in firm endorsement. "The textual messages originated with the women in Amazonia, but all of the imagery transmitted to Joss originates from Maternas."

"Minerva is correct," Demeter and Diana chorus.

Looking flabbergasted, Venus exclaims, "You're asking us to interpret these so-called messages as meaning that our planet is not only a living being but an aware, conscious entity? Minerva," she says earnestly, "you can't possibly—"

"Gaia," I pronounce, and transmit my voice over the hubbub to all the women on this world. "This is proof of what we've always known as Gaia." Hera is behaving exactly in the manner forecast by Mother when she chose to exclude her from our previous discussions. We had not expected Venus to be an ally. Perhaps we should have.

"Gaia is an unprovable *theory*!" Hera shouts.

"Until now. Now we have our proof the theory is true."

"It is true," Joss says.

"Silence," Mother commands over the rising voices. "You will all be quiet."

Only Mother would have such a command instantly obeyed. "Explain, Minerva," she says to me. "From the beginning."

I indeed begin at the beginning. "In ancient mythology, Gaia was the oldest and greatest figure in the pre-classical pantheon of gods: the Earth goddess known for her pitiless punishment of anyone not living in harmony with the living world."

Inspiration strikes, and I turn to Hera. "Perhaps you could explain the theory of Gaia better than I."

Her glance at me is startled, poisonous, and blessedly brief. "I will explain it only with the caveat that while we may wish it to be true, prefer it to be true, Gaia is a *theory* that was first espoused in the twentieth century."

I conceal my smile. I know my sister and that any irritation and disapproval will quickly be submerged as she becomes engaged with the topic and seizes on this opportunity to expound to a planet-wide audience.

"I will concede that we subscribe to many tenets of the Gaia theory. In our reverence for our world and love of her beauty and all her life-forms. And all of us can agree on the concept of homeostasis—"

"Hera," Mother says with an annoyed glance at me, "speak so that even primitive Vernans like myself can understand."

"Yes, Mother," Hera responds respectfully to the wisest one of us all. "Homeostasis is the ability of an organism to maintain internal equilibrium by adjusting its physiological processes."

"Perfectly clear," mutters Mother.

"Both Earth and Maternas have a euphonic ecosystem of oceans where microscopic entities—algae—live. On both planets bacteria are the greater part of life. Like Earth, every cubic centimeter of this world contains billions of organisms—individual forms of life." She raises her voice: "But what is *not* provable is that this planet is itself a sentient being. What is *not* provable is that it has evolved and continues to evolve simply to suit the requirements of its inhabitants. Or that any life-form on this world is able to shape its own environment by simply existing there. Or that everything happening environmentally on this world is a consequence of—not a requirement for—the presence of life."

"The theory of evolution—" Venus begins.

"Argues to some degree against it," Hera speaks over her sister. "Far from having an environment suit itself to them, species become extinct when they don't adapt to environment, when they fail to pass the evolutionary fitness test."

She turns to Diana. "How can you possibly agree with this claim? You're a geneticist—you *know* ultimate selection is not the organism itself but the gene. This would conflict—"

"On Earth," Joss interposes. "Not here."

"Correct," Diana says.

Hera peers at her sister in astonishment. "Diana, we've seen nothing whatever to support this. We've seen no evidence—"

"We have, Hera," Diana says and suddenly there is utter despair in her voice and on her face. "We do see the evidence. It's right before us. The evidence is our children. The children we have lost."

Into a silence that even Hera does not break, Joss says,

"The messages I bring you are from your children and on behalf of your children." She sits with her arms folded on the table before her, head bowed. "They—"

"Joss," Emerald interrupts. Her voice is hushed, her face bleached of color. "Why you? Why you and not me? Or us? When my own daughters were among them, why wouldn't they come to me—"

"Emerald..." Joss, who has previously seemed remote, virtually detached from all these proceedings, looks at her with a compassion that would liquefy a diamond. "They don't because they can't. They're incapable of it. It's obvious in our every contact with them. You have no concept of how far they've moved beyond us. They not only do not speak, they've lost all concept of speech. Lost it by age four. To them we're utterly primitive. They've so surpassed us they're equivalent to humans trying to communicate with an ant or a plant."

"An ant?" Hera says, rising from her seat. "A plant?"

To Joss's astounding information, my sister reacts by choosing to take umbrage at the comparison of her with a plant. I can only shake my head.

"Perhaps a cat or a dog," Joss concedes with perfect seriousness.

Hera sinks back into her chair as if mollified. Again I shake my head.

Venus looks at all of us, at Mother, Megan, myself and my sisters, as if it is up to her to save us from ourselves. "Assuming this is true—and I don't assume it for a moment because we knew before you got here, Joss, that our children have moved into some realm removed from us—you still haven't answered Emerald's question. Why did they choose you to tell all this to?"

"For one reason only: I was able to be a conduit. The women on Amazonia virtually abducted me because I was newly arrived and not of this world."

"Many of us are not of this world," Venus retorts. "Many of us were not born here."

"Unlike you, I was not yet a contaminant—"

"A *contaminant?*" Hera again rises in outrage. "I've heard just about all—"

Joss speaks over her: "Meaning I had not begun any assimilation to this world. I suffered severe disorientation when we landed. I ate no food originating here that would have been absorbed into my Earth-based metabolism to begin poisoning it. The reason your own children consumed soil was because it acted as a decontaminant for the cannibal food given to them—"

"*Cannibal food!*" It is Venus's turn to be outraged.

Joss continues imperturbably, "What I did consume were those flowers on Amazonia—they're what the women there eat and drink, and that nourishment is as pure as mother's milk. I suppose it *is* mother's milk since it's produced directly for your children in a place perfectly suited to them."

"So is our food," Venus retorts. "As chief biologist on this planet, I completely reject your demented accusation of cannibalism. I fail to see any difference between what they and we consume."

"You take living things from this world—"

"Plants!"

"Alien plants, about which you know little."

"We kill no animals—"

"You kill and eat fish."

"The seas teem with them!" Venus breaks off, then says definitively, "I fail to see any difference in practice or in theory between what we eat and they eat."

"There's a drastic difference, esteemed Venus. Maternas provides specific food for your children. Regardless of how we choose to view it, we're predators on this world—we decide what we want and plunder it for those wants."

Joss is confirming what I've always known—that her brilliance as a historian has always been submerged under her profession as a musician.

"We're dominant life-forms," Hera says angrily. "We're by definition predators. But *contaminants?*" She appears far more incensed over this particular term than the substantiation behind what Joss claims. "How can we be such a thing on a world we revere—"

"We're predators and contaminants on both our worlds," Joss says somberly. "Earth as well as Maternas. The difference being that Earth is unable to do anything about us."

"*That* contention utterly fails *any* test of logic," Hera scoffs. "Earth too fits the general definition of Gaia—she is self-regulating, orderly, inexorable. Her tides—"

"Yes," Joss interrupts. "But what is the imagery from Maternas trying to tell us? That she's a living, sentient being, esteemed Hera: a healthy world never damaged by meteors or comets. If anything, it has more optimum conditions for life than Earth, yet no humanoid species has ever come into existence here. Earth was hit by devastating meteor strikes. What the imagery tells us is that Earth was injured so severely that she could do nothing about a life-form she would never otherwise have permitted to exist. The human species arose and managed to reproduce exponentially. Incapable of protecting herself, Earth's entropy deepened, to such a degree she's had no chance of recovering from the human ravages of her."

"Until very recently," I contribute.

"Yes, until the worst of the depredations to that planet came to an end. Even so, it will require millennia if not epochs before she recovers, before our human descendants on Earth meld with her as the children have here on Maternas."

"I see no reason to believe any of this," Hera says, shaking her head. "You yourself wondered if what you imbibed on Amazonia might be an intoxicant. Maybe it was, maybe it produced a hallucinatory—"

"Hera," Mother says, "open your mind beyond your preconceptions. Listen to Joss and Minerva and consider what they present."

If my own experience is any guide, it may take time for women other than Hera to accomplish this, and so Hera's questions and her skepticism are useful—every woman viewing our proceedings needs to understand what has happened and believe in what must be done.

What is conclusive to me from the images presented to Joss and, even more convincingly, from the defection of our children, is that the major force at work is a planet protecting itself from our plunder, however unwitting we were in our behavior. And that while we women have always known to respect and love both our worlds, we have not loved them enough—did not know to do so—and it is now too late.

"You wanted to know who will destroy you." Joss speaks the words that will underscore everything that has happened thus far: "It is Maternas. She has already begun."

"*Why?*" I cannot identify any speakers; too many women have simultaneously said the word.

"Because we don't belong here. Because she doesn't want us here. Because of what we are."

"What we *are*?" Danya leaps to her feet. "We are women who *love* her, who love this world," she shouts. "We've committed none of the atrocities done to Earth. We have ecologists who help us live here in total reverence—"

"We've lived here by our own standards," Joss says calmly.

"The highest of standards!"

"Our own standards," Joss repeats. "With the first generation born here, Maternas began to assimilate your children—"

"Diana—there were no genetic changes," Venus points out, virtually pleading with her sister.

"It doesn't work that way here," Diana responds bleakly.

"No, it doesn't," Joss says. "Not on a healthy world. On

this world three generations of births were all it took for Maternas to assimilate and subsume your children. Three brief generations because each successive one was driven to procreate at an earlier age so Maternas could more easily take them into her and make them her own. You saw the images of them on Amazonia with the animals. They live as the animals do on this world and always will. They have moved well beyond all possibility of retrieval by you."

"This is monstrous," moans Venus. "A tragedy. Such regression—"

"It is tragedy only for us," Joss interrupts Venus. "It is not regression. They've moved light-years beyond us."

"They live in a *jungle.* They live without culture, without art, music, without technology, without..."

She trails off. What has stopped her is the expression on Joss's face.

"Esteemed Venus," Joss says, "they have a consciousness that's melded with that of this planet and all of its creatures. Respectfully, what we have, compared to them, is nothing."

I ask Joss the next question: "Why was it so difficult to transmit messages we could understand? Why did it require sexual experience—"

"Not just sexual experience," Joss says, nodding. "Peak sexual experience: the most elevated and open consciousness we're capable of achieving. Because my body and brain were uncontaminated by anything I consumed, it's where some of these young women could connect and exist with me for the briefest fraction of time. I believe it's a place of rapture where they themselves exist much of the time."

Venus inquires, "While you were there, Joss, how many orgasms did you have?"

Mother sighs with exasperation. Only Venus would ask such a question. Joss responds: "Perhaps three hundred."

Venus shakes her head.

"I believe the women there had more," Joss says. "Not just

when they mate with each other. They seem in a place of rapture when they lie in embrace of the planet."

"Now we have a nongenetic explanation for their unusual development in the genital area," Diana says wryly. "Usage."

"So you're telling us this planet has taken away our children and now wants to destroy us," Venus says in summation.

"The technology we use has made us increasingly unwelcome. The food we seize from this world has made us unwelcome. Our unbridled population growth has made us unwelcome. That more of us have arrived has made us more unwelcome. She will have none of us here, and she is a pitiless Gaia who will destroy us to be rid of us. That we're an inferior and malignant species, that we would never have come into existence even on our own planet except that Earth was too weak to rid herself of us—these are facts we can believe or not, as we wish. Our fate is in our own hands."

As Hera begins to speak, Joss raises both hands to stop her. "The earthquakes striking Femina are not anomalies. That they are becoming more and more severe is obvious. It's only a matter of time before technology cannot protect us. Like that ancient goddess Gaia, Maternas will tear herself open and swallow us if that's what it takes to be finally rid of us. The children you've lost know they cannot protect us and are desperate to warn us. They have sent me here to warn you—"

"Is that why they all came back here when you landed?" The question is from Emerald.

Joss nods. "I believe so. They knew the arrival of more of us meant the end."

"And that strange gathering around Mother's house?"

"It was acknowledgement of us all as their progenitors and recognition of her as the genesis of them all—"

"Just as you suggested, Danya," I say.

"Another reason was to urgently find someone. My sister's

descendants at the landing—they took my hands. I believe that's how they knew I was…viable. Any of us new to this world might have been taken for the same purpose, had I not been accidentally delivered to them."

Joss looks at us around the table and says, "A question none of you has asked is how, without technology, so many thousands of them managed to travel to Femina."

"They did use technology," Hera says triumphantly. "They got here the same way you did."

"I did use a flitter. Unlike them."

"Now you're telling us they can move themselves anywhere at will," Venus says, rolling her eyes.

"They must," Joss says. "They have absolutely no technology."

"You've actually seen this?"

"No. They don't physically move around much at all. I can only infer it. How else did they get here? And back?"

"Joss." Emerald speaks. "What about my daughter? What about Adira? What about all our daughters of her generation?"

"I believe I can offer an answer," I say, and I speak to every woman on this world. "Vesta now believes that all of your daughters in that transitional generation are gone, dead of their own volition. Because they knew they belonged neither with you nor with children who had all become daughters of Maternas."

Some time later, as smothered sobs continue, as we try to digest all this news, Tara speaks for the first time. And asks the key question.

"For those of us who believe this is true, what do we do now?"

"My dears," Mother answers softly, "what we must do is leave."

"This has been our home for decades. A home we love," Venus mourns.

"A home no longer ours. Whether we believe Joss doesn't actually matter. Our children are lost to us for whatever the reason, and we can bring no more children into a world where we will only lose them. This is no longer a home for us, and we must leave it. Immediately."

PERSONAL JOURNAL OF MINERVA ONBOARD THE FOREMOTHER

In the turbulent weeks since the revelation of Joss's experiences on Amazonia to our entire Sisterhood, I have been far too occupied with my part in making history to devote any time to assessing it. Until this day.

Our planet-wide priority—to respond immediately to the dire warning Joss conveyed to us—has resulted in perhaps the most frenetic and productive time of our entire presence on this world.

The first logical step was to evacuate Cybele. But where to? We would not be remotely welcome anywhere on the planet. Our obvious option, Earth, was not immediately feasible, not with only the *Connie Esperanza* outfitted for interstellar travel and incapable of holding our ten thousand even with maximum expansion of her passenger capacity.

Modifying other existing transport ships brought its own dilemma because we could no longer expropriate resources from a planet we now understood to be both sentient and balefully inimical to our every act.

Megan provided immediate solutions: "We have more than enough ships capable of planetary orbit to hold us all. Let's first get ourselves into them and off the surface while we safely can. We can take minimal plant cuttings and refit the drones as fast-growth hydroponic chambers. We have sufficient food supplies till then."

Hera came up with another key approach: "We'll put our synthesizers aboard the *Connie* and take her on a search for regolith—"

"What, pray tell, is regolith?" I demanded.

"Rock rubble. We'll mine any we find orbiting non life-bearing planets. And get ourselves quickly away from here."

It was then that Mother grumbled, "I have to live in space *again*. And this time who knows for how long..."

Of all of us, she seems to suffer most during our interstellar sojourns—or perhaps she is merely the most vocal complainant. In her advancing years she has become more needful of physical comfort along with intellectual stimulus.

Vesta hastened to reassure her. "We'll do our best to provide diversions, Mother. Our libraries will be transferred in their entirety. Holograms of our art. Your favorite musicians will be yours for the asking. I'll personally verify we have the best exemplars for every food you prefer—"

Mother raised a hand, acknowledging these guarantees with a mollified nod. And a request: "Since we'll in planetary orbit for some weeks, perhaps I could have a room with a view."

Which we have provided.

Under Hera's command, the *Connie*'s probes quickly identified an asteroid belt particularly rich in the heavy minerals our ships' sheathing requires, and we put our synthesizers to work. Having acquired considerable expertise after outfitting three previous voyages, we melded the *Sarah Bernhardt, Marie Curie,* and *Eleanor Roosevelt* into one cavernous vessel—this one—which we have renamed *Foremother*. We overhauled her propulsion systems, and with our entire complement of women concentrated full time on the task, progressed rapidly in reinforcing her shields to make her spaceworthy.

Cybele… What has happened to Cybele has served to corroborate beyond all question our interpretation of Joss's visions while at the same time grieving our souls. From the moment we evacuated the planet, daily earthquakes rocked Femina, with such ferocity in Cybele in particular, that all of our homes and structures there, along with every other vestige of our presence, are being reduced to dust, leaving us to ponder whether only some unimaginable effort of intercession on the part of our newest generations managed to save it and us from a much earlier fate. What is certain is that on a planet so ruthlessly determined to erase our every trace, future explorers from other worlds, other galaxies—should there ever be any—will find no evidence that humankind as we presently define it was ever here.

Hera is by no means humbled by this dramatic repudiation of her arguments against Joss's warnings, having decided to interpret her exclusion from our discussions with Joss her own way. "Brilliant strategy," she avowed, "allowing me to present credible challenges to Joss's messages and visions."

Joss. To her my thoughts go constantly.

Up to this very moment she remains on Amazonia. We can retrieve her at any time up to the last few minutes before we depart from orbit. Will she call on us? Before it's irretrievably too late?

This is what I know of her. Since we presented to the Unity only the messages and visions relevant to us, Olympia has taken precious time away from her reunion with Ceeley and joined with me in viewing, reflecting upon, and discussing all that Joss brought back on her recorder of her experiences. We are the only ones who know what transpired between Joss and the women of Amazonia beyond when the messages meant for us ceased.

We know there is someone who is meaningful to Joss, who first appeared during the second night when the five women came to Joss. The voluptuous, goddess-like woman who was the first to offer her own desire to Joss, to receive pleasure from her.

Our knowledge is limited and speculative, because after Emerald's departure, Joss's recorder ceased to be the sublimely informative instrument it had been when integrated with the dual prisms of her personality and her analytic thought. When she was not receiving the visions, her recorder held only the basics of experience, as if she had disconnected, had completely switched off every aspect of herself and become a mere camera. But her feeling for this particular woman was transparent, her every viewing of her through a heated glow of desire.

The first one occurred the day after Emerald left. That morning, Joss again accompanied the women down from the plateau and witnessed their communal time with the animals. Afterward, she saw this magnificent goddess again. And gazed at her in utter admiration and longing.

The woman slowly turned to her like a flower to the sun, looked at her with her ethereal coral eyes. Came to her, took Joss's face in her hands and tenderly kissed her. Then, while still kissing her, picked her up and carried her off to a nearby cluster of trees. Placed the astonished Joss down on a carpet of ferns. Lowered herself gently onto her, and fitted Joss's body to hers. Began an endless tide of diverse pleasures, with Joss's legs quivering around her. The next hour or so brought rapture and ecstasies, until Joss lay under her limp and replete.

Again she picked up Joss and carried her. Back to where her companions lay in their daily communion with their world. Placed her down and assumed her own position spread-eagled alongside them, and Joss fell into a sweet sleep beside her.

Joss's ensuing nights were an orgiastic fever involving many different women, no two the same, as she received her messages and imagery. But each and every day below the plateau Joss's recorder contained an hour, sometimes more, of this goddess in her arms, and her ardent and fulsome possession of Joss amid the ferns, an ardor undiminished over the four weeks the recordings lasted. For the two nights before Joss understood the visions had definitively ended and that she must return to us with the recorder, the woman found Joss each night and they fused in a mutual fire of consummation until other women wishing to take their pleasures intervened, and only then did they relinquish each other.

Since what we view is only through the limited lens of Joss herself, I have no idea what this may mean in a realm so removed from our own concepts, no idea whether this liaison will endure—indeed, whether it is rare or commonplace among all the women there. I only know that it is so intense and profoundly beautiful that I cannot imagine Joss choosing to leave it. Or leaving this world.

Others, however, having no knowledge of this, disagree on principle, and confidently expect her to rejoin us. Such as Venus. It has escaped no one, especially Venus, that Joss personifies the kind of sensual existence that Venus has always symbolized. And so I have asked her: "Have you considered remaining here in the manner that Joss now does?"

"Of course, Minerva," she replied with a trace of impatience. "How they live and love proves what I've always believed all women are capable of. But," and she ticked off a list on her fingers, "I have deep emotional connections with Mother and my sisters of the Inner Circle, and none of you would join me. I'm far less flexible than young Joss when it comes to the comforts technology brings. Most of all, I can't imagine a world without speech, without the culture that I know, especially when I have no means of reaching the sphere they inhabit. Minerva," she said, looking at me earnestly, "it's for that last reason Joss must and will return to us. She is at her core one of us, not one of them: a musician who needs to create her music. She belongs with us, not with them."

I do not know Olympia's feelings, but after much reflection, in resignation and sorrow I have come to the private belief that Venus is wrong and that Joss does belong with them and is lost to us. I believe she has managed to retain and perhaps expand the higher consciousness opened in her by the women of Amazonia, and her inclusion in every aspect of their physical lives is the best indication that what I theorize is true. I believe she disconnected herself from her recorder because she now sees and is part of their music, and their music is the music of the spheres.

We will soon know. Our ships' commanders have begun the operational sequence to take us out of orbit, and Joss's decision will soon be irrevocable...

I am Minerva the historian, and, knowing that my philosopher sister Olympia will be far more sagacious in her observations and eloquent in her reflections in these final minutes, I conclude my chronicle of our Sisterhood on Maternas.

PERSONAL JOURNAL OF OLYMPIA ONBOARD THE FOREMOTHER

I confess I have been far too happily preoccupied with my reunion with Ceeley for much attention to this journal. Until now. Until this final, momentous, emotional day.

After the extraordinarily high stress and perilous conditions that brought Ceeley and me back together, our renewed love seems infinitely sweeter than it did so many years ago, even though we were then so much younger; it feels deeper and more gratifying now. Intimacy with her has returned me to adolescence and that tumbling eagerness to share every meaningful experience during our separation. But we come up against the strange, even ludicrous circumstance of six years having passed in my Earth life, while fifty-five have gone by in hers.

In our previous relationship on Earth I was by far the more mature; now we are virtually contemporaries in both years and life experience. Yet in some ways my six Earth years held more drama and peril and adventure than most of Ceeley's time on Maternas, which was tranquil and idyllic. On the other hand, aside from my unremitting longing for her, I have suffered far less personal sorrow. Her most recent years on this world have brought her, as they have to so many others, the grievous defection of precious descendants, a loss only partly ameliorated by Joss's discoveries. Ceeley speaks little of the intervening love relationships from which she drew comfort during my absence, and I have none whatever to report. I do not remotely begrudge her any happiness she may have found with another within the chasm of our years apart; I feel too grateful for the blessing of having a bridge to those years and for having her restored to me.

Another joy: At the end of the journey that will soon begin, I will have another precious being added to my abundance of blessings. My sister Isis, restored to me.

And Hera has raised the fascinating idea that a new route she is charting back through the time warp may hold the possibility of reversing time and may equalize some of our age distortions when we arrive on Earth. It is only a hope, but still a hope.

Amid these joys and hopes, I am suffering deep loss. We of the Inner Circle and our closest loved ones are gathered in the command cabin of the *Foremother,* moments away from leaving orbit, from leaving Maternas forever. And Joss has sent us no signal. It is clear that this young woman so precious to me will remain on Maternas and be forever lost to me.

And to Emerald. And to Tara. Emerald faces her loss with calm dignity; she seems to have reached a stage of acceptance. She comforts Tara, holding her hand; these too have grown very close in the commonality of their loss.

Even as we weep for the loss of this world and those who remain here, we realize that there are consolations.

For Joss and for all the daughters of Maternas, theirs will be a world of everlasting pristine beauty and untold richness unfolding under coral skies and all the brilliant tapestries of night.

For us who leave, we return to the vibrant green forests and restless green-blue seas that envelop the healing heart and soul of Earth. We return to our true home–a necessary return, beyond what has happened here, because of the urgency of the message we bear. Earth is not only the mother of us all; she is far more a living mother than we ever knew, and there is remedial work we must all do. There are whole new areas of study we must open for her sake and for ours…

Wait—wait. Something *astonishing* is happening.

Something impossible.

Were my sisters all around me not exclaiming and pointing, I would think I was hallucinating.

Outside the windows of the *Foremother* are the coral-eyed daughters of Amazonia. Thousands. Impossibly, they float in space hand in hand around *Foremother,* around the *Connie Esperanza.*

"A projection," Hera whispers, a hand at her throat.

"No matter," Mother says, her face streaming with tears. "They're here. To say farewell."

I understand how wrenching this must be for Mother. Her dream of a home in the stars, a world of only women, has brought an outcome no one could have imagined.

I cling to Minerva. I too am in tears—we all are.

The countdown ends. We ease from orbit, away from these daughters of Maternas, and begin our journey home to Earth.

We need Mother to speak to us now. We, her daughters, all of us, need her. And speak to us she does:

"My dear ones, we leave a beautiful world at peace with itself. We return to an Earth also at peace—for the first time in its recorded history.

"The dream of our Sisterhood has always been to provide for our daughters a healthy, safe, and better world.

"We will bequeath to them two such worlds."

ABOUT THE AUTHOR

Two-time Lambda Literary Award winner Katherine V. Forrest is the author of the lesbian romantic classic *Curious Wine* as well as the groundbreaking Kate Delafield mystery series that includes the best-sellers *Murder by Tradition*, *Amateur City*, *Sleeping Bones*, and *Hancock Park*. She lives in San Francisco.